The Emissary

Also by Yoko Tawada

AVAILABLE FROM NEW DIRECTIONS

Yoko Tawada

The Emissary

Translated from the Japanese
by Margaret Mitsutani

A NEW DIRECTIONS PAPERBOOK ORIGINAL

New Directions gratefully acknowledges the support
of The Japan Foundation.

JAPANFOUNDATION

Originally published in Japanese as *Kentoshi* by Kodansha

Manufactured in the United States of America
New Directions Books are printed on acid-free paper
First published as a New Directions Paperbook in 2018

Library of Congress Cataloging-in-Publication Data
Names: Tawada, Yōko, 1960– author. | Mitsutani, Margaret, translator.
Title: The emissary / Yoko Tawada ; translated by Margaret Mitsutani.
Other titles: Kentoshi. English
Description: New York : New Directions, 2018.
Identifiers: LCCN 2017041786 (print) | LCCN 2017048878 (ebook) |
ISBN 9780811227636 | ISBN 9780811227629 (acid-free paper)
Classification: LCC PL862.A85 (ebook) |
LCC PL862.A85 K4613 2018 (print) | DDC 895.6/35—dc23
LC record available at https://lccn.loc.gov/2017041786

4 6 8 10 9 7 5 3

New Directions Books are published for James Laughlin
by New Directions Publishing Corporation
80 Eighth Avenue, New York 10011

The Emissary

STILL IN HIS BLUE SILK PAJAMAS, MUMEI SAT WITH his bottom flat on the tatami. Perhaps it was his head, much too large for his slender long neck, that made him look like a baby bird. Hairs fine as silk threads stuck to his scalp, damp with sweat. His eyes nearly shut, he moved his head as if searching the air, trying to catch on his tympanic membrane the scraping of footsteps on gravel. The footsteps grew louder, then stopped. The sliding door rattled like a freight train, and as Mumei opened up his eyes, morning light, yellow as melted dandelions, poured in. The boy threw back his shoulders, puffed out his chest and stuck out both his arms like a bird spreading its wings.

Smiling, deep wrinkles around his eyes, Yoshiro came closer, his shoulders heaving. No sooner had he lowered his head, lifting a foot to take off a shoe, than beads of sweat dripped from his forehead.

Every morning, Yoshiro rented a dog from the Rent-a-Dog place on the corner to run with along the riverbank for about half an hour. When the water level was low, the river looked like silver ribbons that stretched out much further than you'd expect. Long ago, this sort of purposeless running had been referred to as *jogging*, but with foreign words falling out of use, it was now called *loping down*, an expression that had started out as a joke meaning "if you lope your blood pressure goes down," but everybody called it that these days. And kids Mumei's age would never have dreamt that adding just an *e* in front of it the word *lope* could conjure up visions of a young woman climbing down a ladder in the middle of the night to run away with her lover.

Yet even now, when foreign words were rarely used, the walls of the Rent-a-Dog store were still plastered with the katakana script used to write them. When Yoshiro had just started loping down and wasn't sure how much speed he could manage, he'd first rented a Yorkshire terrier, thinking a small dog might better, but then he'd found it much too fast. He'd stumbled, almost falling, gasping for breath as the dog pulled him along, turning its head now and then, cheekily holding its snout high with a self-satisfied air as if to say, "How's that for speed?" The following morning he'd tried a dachshund that turned out to be so lazy it had sunk to the ground after the first two hundred yards or so, forcing Yoshiro to drag it all the way back to the Rent-a-Dog place.

"Some dogs sure don't like to go for a walk," he'd griped as he returned the animal.

"A what? A walk? Oh, yeah, a walk, ha, ha, ha," laughed the man behind the counter, finally catching on. It was a superior sort of laugh, directed at this old geezer who still used outdated expressions like *a walk*. The shelf life of words was getting shorter all the time—it wasn't only the foreign ones that were falling out of use. And some words that had disappeared after being labeled "old-fashioned" had no heirs to take their place.

A week before he'd rented a German shepherd, which had been just the opposite of the dachshund; in fact, that dog was so well trained he made Yoshiro feel inferior. Yoshiro could run at top speed until he was so exhausted he'd be dragging his feet, barely moving, but whatever the pace, the shepherd stayed with him, right at his side. When Yoshiro looked at him the dog would flash back a glance as if to say, "How am I doing? Perfect, wouldn't you say?" Disgusted by all this exactitude, Yoshiro firmly resolved never to rent another German shepherd.

So Yoshiro had never found his ideal dog, and yet when the man behind the counter asked "Which breed do you prefer?" he was secretly pleased with himself, the way he hemmed and hawed, unable to come up with a reply.

In his youth, Yoshiro had prided himself on always having an answer ready when someone asked who his favorite composer or designer was, or what kind of wine he preferred. Confident in his good taste, he had poured time and money into surrounding himself with things that would show it off. Now he no longer felt any need to use taste as the bricks and mortar for a structure called "individuality." Though shoes were still important, he no longer chose them as a means of asserting his identity. The *Idaten* shoes he was now wearing were a new line recently marketed by the Tengu Company—extremely comfortable, they resembled straw sandals. The Tengu Company was based in Iwate Prefecture, and inside each shoe *Iwate* was written in India ink with a brush, followed by the kana for *ma* and *de*.* The younger generation, who no longer studied English, interpreted the "made" on old "Made in Japan" labels in their own way.

* The Japanese word *made* (pronounced mah-day) means "to" or "until," so *Iwate made* would mean "to Iwate."

In high school, his feet had seemed almost like foreign appendages the way they kept on growing, leaving the rest of his body behind, with soft, easily punctured skin that made him seek out brand-name foreign shoes to keep them covered with thick, hard rubber. While working for the company he'd joined after university, he had always worn heavy brown leather shoes to hide the fact that he didn't intend to stick around very long. After publishing his first novel, he had spent part of the royalties on a pair of hiking boots. Before leaving home, even if he was only going to the neighborhood post office, he would lace them up tight in case he got stranded somewhere.

It wasn't until he was past seventy that his feet felt happiest in wooden or straw sandals. This sort of footwear left his insteps exposed to rain and mosquitoes, yet as he gazed down at the bare skin, quietly enduring all these dangers, he thought, "These feet are just like me," and a desire to run welled up inside him. He'd been looking for something akin to straw sandals when he came across these shoes, made by Tengu, Inc.

Stumbling as he took his shoes off, Yoshiro rested a hand on the wooden pillar to steady himself, feeling the grain of the wood under his fingers. The years are recorded in rings inside the trunk of a tree, but how was time recorded in his own body? Time didn't spread out gradually, ring after ring, nor was it lined up neatly in a row; could it just be a disorderly pile, like the inside of a drawer no one ever bothers to straighten? The thought made him stumble again; this time he put his left foot down to steady himself.

"Seems I'm still not very good at standing on one leg," he

muttered to himself, prompting Mumei to scrunch up his eyes, lifting his nose slightly as he asked, "Great-grandpa, are you trying to be a crane?" The moment he spoke, the boy's head, which had been bobbing around gently like a balloon, abruptly stopped, settling into its proper place on top of his spinal cord as a mischievous, sweetly sour look appeared in his eyes. For a moment, his great-grandson looked so much like a little Buddha it rattled Yoshiro, leading him to bark in as harsh a tone as he could manage "Are you still in your pajamas? Hurry up and get dressed!" He yanked open the dresser drawer, where the child's underwear and school clothes, neatly folded into a square the night before, were patiently awaitng their master's call. Mumei always worried about his clothes, afraid they'd get up and leave in the middle of the night. He'd be beside himself, picturing his shirt downing cocktails in some nightclub, his trousers dancing up a storm until they finally traipsed back home, dirty and wrinkled. Which was why Yoshiro always made sure they were safely locked up in the drawer before he went to bed.

"Get dressed by yourself—I'm not helping you this time."

Plunking the clothes down in front of his great-grandson, Yoshiro went to the bathroom to splash his face clean with cold water. Wiping his face with a thin Japanese cotton towel, he stared at the wall in front of him. There was no mirror. He wondered how long it had been since he had seen his own image. Until he was in his eighties, he had checked his face every morning, trimming his nose hairs if they were too long, putting camellia salve on the wrinkles at the corners of his eyes if the skin was dry.

Yoshiro draped the little towel over the laundry pole in the garden, securing it with a clothespin. He wasn't sure when they had stopped using plush, Western-style bath towels. They'd taken so long to dry there were never enough. Japanese-style towels, on the other hand, were so thin and light you could just hang them over the pole where they'd catch the wind, flapping gently and before you knew it they were dry. Long ago Yoshiro had been in thrall to those huge, heavy bath towels. Every time he used one he would stick it in the washing machine, tossing handfuls of laundry detergent in after it, but those days now seemed like a joke. Spinning all those heavy towels around in its belly was agony for the poor washing machine—each one would die of sheer exhaustion after a few years. Hundreds of thousands of dead washing machines had sunk to the bottom of the Pacific Ocean to become capsule hotels for fish.

Sandwiched in between the eight-mat room and the kitchen was a room with a wooden floor about six and a half feet wide in which a light foldout picnic table and folding chairs like the ones anglers use were set up. As if to add to the gay summer excursion atmosphere, on the table was a thermos emblazoned with a picture of a raccoon dog with a huge dandelion sticking out of it.

Recently all dandelions had petals at least four inches long. Someone had even submitted one of these jumbo dandelions to the annual Chrysanthemum Show at the Civic Center, giving rise to a debate over whether it should be recognized as a chrysanthemum. "Oversized dandelions are not chrysanthemums—merely mutations," asserted one faction, while another charged that "mutation" was a pejorative term, further enflaming the war of words. Actually, the word *mutation* was rarely used anymore, having been replaced by the more popular *environmental adaptation*. With most plants growing larger and larger, if the dandelion alone had stayed small it would have ended up like a kept woman, hiding away in the shadows. It had simply grown larger in order to survive in this new environment. Yet there were other plants that had chosen to survive by getting smaller. A new species of bamboo, no larger than a person's little finger when fully grown, had been named "the pinky bamboo." With trees this small, if the Moon Princess from the Woodcutter's Tale came down to earth again to be discovered shining inside a bamboo, the old man and woman would have to crawl on their hands and knees peering through magnifying glasses to find her.

Among the anti-dandelion faction were those who said, "The chrysanthemum, that noble flower chosen for the Imperial crest, cannot be put in the same category as a weed." Whereupon the Dandelion Support Association, comprised mainly of members of the Brotherhood of Ramen Workers, fired back with the famous Imperial decree that "There is no such thing as a weed," which finally silenced their enemies, ending the seven-month-long Chrysanthemum-Dandelion controversy.

For Yoshiro, one look at a dandelion was enough to bring back childhood memories of lying in a grassy field gazing up at the sky. The air was warm, the grass cool. He heard birds chirping far away. Turning his head to one side, he would see a dandelion in bloom, looming just slightly above his eyes. Sometimes he would stick out his lips like a bird's beak to give it a kiss, then suddenly sit up, looking around to make sure no one had seen.

Mumei had never once played in a real field. Even so, he seemed to have an image of a field he carefully cultivated in his mind.

"Let's buy some paint for the walls," he had said suddenly, several weeks earlier. Not catching his meaning, Yoshiro had asked, "The walls? They're still clean enough, don't you think?"

"We can paint them blue, like the sky. With pictures of clouds, and birds, too."

"You want to have a picnic indoors?"

"Well, we can't have one outside, can we?"

Yoshiro swallowed hard. In a few years' time, perhaps, they would no longer able to leave the house, and would have to be satisfied with a life surrounded by outdoor scenes painted on walls. Trying his best to look happy, he replied, "Good idea. I'll see if I can find some blue paint." If the idea of living under virtual house arrest hadn't occurred to Mumei, there was no need to destroy his innocence.

Because he didn't get along with chairs very well, Mumei always took his meals sitting cross-legged on the tatami, eating from a lacquer tray with a swirling design of the famous Naruto whirlpool. He appeared to be playing make-believe, acting the role of a feudal lord. He also did his homework sitting on the tatami at his low desk by the window. Even so, he protested vehemently whenever Yoshiro said, "Since we don't really use the table and chairs, why don't we give them away?" Mumei may not have needed them as furniture, yet the table and chairs inspired him, calling forth images of a long forgotten time, or of faraway lands that he would probably never visit.

The paraffin wrapping sounded like a sudden shower when Yoshiro peeled it back to get out a loaf of rye bread. It was Shikoku-style German bread, charred the color of midnight and heavy as granite. The crust was hard and dry, the inside soft and moist. This faintly sour black bread was called "Aachen," written with Chinese characters that meant "Pseudo Opium." The baker had named each variety of bread he baked after a German city, which he wrote in Chinese characters with roughly the same pronunciation, so that Hanover meant "Blade's Aunt," Bremen "Wobbly Noodles," and Rothenberg "Outdoor Hot Springs Haven." The poster on the bakery door said, "So many kinds of bread. Seek out the one that suits your taste," a hollow slogan that got on Yoshiro's linguistic nerves, yet looking at the baker's thick, doughy earlobes always brought back his sense of trust. They would no doubt be delicious kneaded and baked; the longer you chewed, the sweeter they would taste. The baker was "young elderly," a phrase that had once cracked people up but was now standard usage. People weren't even called "middle-aged elderly" nowadays until they were well into their nineties, and the baker was barely into his late seventies.

Wanting to linger on your futon a few minutes past the time you have to get up is perhaps only human; if so, there was nothing human about this baker. Every morning at exactly four o'clock, without the aid of an alarm clock, he leapt out of bed like a jack-in-the-box propelled by a tightly coiled spring. Then, striking a match four inches long, he lit a candle, two inches in diameter and four inches tall, which he put in a candle holder to light the way as he stepped into his pitch-black kitchen. Though he worked there every day, each morning he felt as taut and determined as if he were entering a sacred temple for the first time. He could tell from a slight warmth in the air that while he was asleep, someone in this very space had added yeast to invisible dough, let it rise, then lovingly baked it for him. He was sure that it was this invisible night bread—bread that would never be sold—that made his daytime bread possible. Its warmth and aroma were gone in moments, and although he never saw who baked the night bread, he was certain it was this mysterious being that kept him from feeling lonely as he started his solitary work.

Because the bakery opened at 6:15 a.m. and closed at 6:45 p.m. some people suspected that the baker had once worked in a school, but this schedule was simply the result of his having measured the time each separate task in the bakery took, starting from 4:00 a.m. when he got up. If a corporation decides its employees are to start work at 8:30 a.m. they all have to be there, sleepy or not, but the baker followed rules he had made up himself.

The bakery had one other employee who, like Yoshiro, was over a hundred years old. A small man, he darted about the shop like a weasel. As Yoshiro was watching him one day, the baker approached to whisper in his ear, "He's my uncle. Says anyone over a hundred doesn't need to rest anymore. When I ask him if he'd like to break for tea he gets mad and yells, 'Young people these days spend more time on breaks than they do working.' Scolds me for even suggesting it."

Nodding vigorously, Yoshiro replied, "Old people have always complained about the young—seems to be good for them—take an old man's blood pressure after he's gone on about kids today for a while—it's always lower than before."

Looking enviously at Yoshiro, elderly enough to dispense with adjectives like "young" or "middle-aged," the young-elderly baker said, "Actually, my uncle's blood pressure is lower than mine. Doesn't take medicine either. You look like yours is low, too. Watching my uncle work it's hard to believe that youngsters used to retire in their sixties."

"Retirement—what an odd system, but it was important back then, as a way of handing jobs over to younger people."

"A long time ago, when I was a painter, it made me kind of proud to think I could never retire."

"So you gave up painting?"

"Yes. I used to paint landscapes in oils, but some art critic would write, 'This scene definitely looks like the Swiss Alps' or something, and that always got me worried. No matter what I painted, somebody would think it was a foreign place. Downright scary. I decided to take cover in the family business, and now I'm here for good, baking bread. Of course bread originally came from Europe, but for some reason it's still allowed."

"To think people used to say French bread, and even English bread ... Sounds so Japanese now—really takes you back, doesn't it?"

Yoshiro had lowered his voice when mentioning foreign

countries and, glancing around to make sure no one was listening, the baker said, "Actually, we used to call this German bread. Officially it's Sanuki bread now ... people don't seem to remember that *bread* is a foreign word."

"Bread reminds you of faraway lands—that they exist, I mean—that's what I like about it. I'd rather eat rice, but bread sets you dreaming. So keep up the good work."

"Sure thing. But you know baking bread is hard work. I'm always straining my muscles, or maybe my tendons even. My arms feel so heavy when I'm lying down. Sometimes I wish I could detach them when I go to bed at the shoulder like a robot."

"There's a class on how to loosen up, you know. I saw an ad for it a while ago. They're holding it at the aquarium. You reminded me of it when you mentioned *tendons* just now, because the Chinese character for *octopus* looks so much like it."

"Oh yeah, I saw that poster too. *Learn to Limber Up from the Octopus.*"

"Yeah, that's the one. I used to think stretching to limber up was nonsense, but you know, the human race may be evolving in a direction no one ever imagined. I mean, maybe we're moving toward the octopus. Watching my great-grandson I certainly get that impression."

"So in another hundred thousand years we'll all be octopi?"

"Maybe so. People always thought of that as devolution, but it might just be evolution after all."

"In high school I used to envy people with bodies like Greek statues. I was trying to get into art school, you see. Don't know when I developed a liking for entirely different bodies—birds, say, or octopi. I'd like to see everything from an optical point of view."

"Optical?"

"No, I meant octopi. I want to see through the eyes of an octopus."

Remembering his conversation with the baker, Yoshiro waited for the soy milk he had poured into a small saucepan to heat up. Mumei's teeth were so soft he couldn't eat bread unless it was softened by steeping.

When he had seen Mumei's baby teeth drop out one after another like pomegranate pulp, leaving his mouth smeared with blood, Yoshiro had been so distressed he'd wandered aimlessly around the house for a while, not knowing what to do. After trying to calm the waves of anxiety that crashed in his heart by telling himself that, after all, milk teeth were meant to be lost, he had finally put Mumei on the back of his bicycle and headed for the dentist's office. Since they didn't have an appointment they were kept waiting for over two hours. In the humid waiting room Yoshiro had crossed and recrossed his legs, pulling at his eyebrows or bringing two fingers to his lips as if smoking a cigarette as he looked up at the clock again and again. There were some oversized model teeth in the waiting room. Mumei took a large model wisdom tooth and put it down on the floor, pushing it along the red carpet like a toy truck. Imagining a world without people, where huge teeth had turned into trucks to roam the highways, Yoshiro shuddered.

Having tired of playing with model teeth, Mumei was now leafing through the pages of a large picture book he had spread across his knees, called *Mr. Canine Tooth's Adventure*. Yoshiro peered over, not sure whether he wanted to read along or not. At the time he had been writing a children's book. He wanted to write something Mumei would be able to read, but at the same time, Mumei's presence made it difficult to write for children. A raw, honest treatment of the problems they faced every day would only end in frustration at the absence of solutions, making it impossible to arrive at places one could only reach in books. Creating an ideal fictional world for his great-grandson was another possibility, although reading about an ideal world wouldn't help the boy change the world around him any time soon.

Mumei gazed down at the book with moist, dewy eyes. The cast of characters included Mr. Canine Tooth, the hero, along with Miss Wisdom Tooth, Mr. Front Tooth, Little Miss Cavity, and Mr. Gold Filling. When his owner falls down, Mr. Canine Tooth, slammed against the concrete, cracks off and falls into a sewer. Though the rats don't know what to think of him at first, they eventually make him into a god, installing him in his own shrine. Worshipped as the god of the underworld, Mr. Canine Tooth manages to preside over festivals for each of the four seasons until the sewer is flooded in a heavy rain, which washes the shrine away and returns Mr. Canine Tooth to the world above, where a child picks him up, puts him in his pocket, and takes him home. At which point the nurse called Yoshiro and Mumei.

"Fall out," Yoshiro mumbled before the dentist had a chance to speak. Still flustered, hoping the dentist didn't think he'd said *fallout*, he quickly corrected himself. "They fell out of his mouth," adding almost as an afterthought, "his baby teeth, I mean." That was a subject-verb inversion, he was thinking when Mumei grinned, having come up with an inversion of his own: "They fell down, my grades I mean."

"Baby teeth are meant to be lost so it's natural, I suppose, but I was shocked at how easily his came out," Yoshiro explained. "Teeth usually put up a real fight to stay in, don't they? So why should his just pop out that way, or am I worrying too much?" he went on, sounding more and more desperate as his voice trailed off. The dentist replied coolly, "Any weakness in the milk teeth carries over to the permanent teeth." Though this verdict made Yoshiro feel as if a huge boulder had just been sewn inside his chest, Mumei, with the curiosity of a budding scientist asked, "What good are milk teeth in the first place, if they're meant to be lost?" The dentist patiently answered his question before beginning his examination. And then, when the dentist was finished, the boy came out with, "Thank you for treating my teeth so kindly." This overly polite expression of gratitude made Yoshiro's stomach flip over. Where could the boy have picked up such a foreign-sounding sentence, when books— even picture books—were no longer being translated? It was utterly mysterious.

Like most children of his generation, Mumei was unable to absorb the calcium he needed. Human beings may turn into a toothless species someday, Yoshiro thought, mulling over what the dentist had said on their way home until Mumei—responding to his unspoken anxiety—chirped, "Don't worry, Great-grandpa, sparrows get along fine without teeth, you know." Mumei had an uncanny ability to read people's thoughts. It spooked Yoshiro sometimes, the way he didn't just sense a person's general mood, but actually seemed to read their minds, as if he were reading a book. Though he tried not to think the worst about Mumei's future, he often found himself sick with worry, with high tides of misery sweeping over him day and night.

"You manage to eat plenty without teeth, Great-grandpa, and look how healthy you are."

Yoshiro was still sunk beneath waves of anxiety, and here was Mumei, trying to cheer him up. That his great-grandson's mental development consisted mainly of coming up with ever-new ways to comfort an old man made Yoshiro feel guilty. If only the boy would be a little more self-centered, do crazy things, live freely ...

To get a little more calcium into Mumei, for a while Yoshiro had tried giving him about half a cup of milk every morning, but the boy's body had responded with diarrhea. The dentist explained that diarrhea is the intestines' method of getting rid of whatever they decide is poisonous as quickly and efficiently as possible. The brain in the head is well known, the dentist went on, but the intestines are actually another brain, and when these two brains disagree the intestines always get the upper hand. This is why the brain is sometimes called the Upper House, and the intestines the Lower House. Because Lower House elections are held often, it is generally believed that it's the Lower House that truly reflects shifts in public opinion. In the same way, because the contents of the intestines are constantly changing, the intestines reflect a person's physical condition more accurately than the brain.

Mumei's mouth apparently won't open all by itself, for when the dentist says, "Open wide!" his eyes and mouth respond simultaneously. Once, when his mouth opened so wide he nearly dislocated his jaw, he quickly shut it, then closed both eyes and said, "The earth is in the back of my throat," before opening his mouth and eyes again, as wide as before. He had mentioned "the earth" once before, during his physical at the pediatric clinic. After rolling up his undershirt to stick out his chest, so thin every rib showed, he calmly announced, "The earth is inside this chest." Turning away to hide his surprise, Yoshiro had looked up, pretending he was observing the trees outside, and grinned.

As *physical* sounded too much like *phthisical*, a word associated with asthma, tuberculosis, and death, the phrase *physical examination* had fallen out of use, with many doctors preferring to call it *the monthly look-over*. The pediatrician would begin by carefully examining a child's tongue and throat, after which the eyelids were pulled back to check the eyes. The skin on the palms of the hands, the face, the neck and back were given a thorough going-over, one hair was pulled out to be sent for analysis, and a light was shone into the ears and nose.

"You're trying to find out how far cellular destruction has gone, aren't you?" Yoshiro one time had asked, unable to suppress his anxiety.

"That's right," the doctor had answered with a grin, "but we can't just put some cells into a machine and come up with actual numbers to show us that and any doctor who tries to tell you we can is a fraud. What we really have to look at is the whole body."

This pediatrician, Dr. Satori, was distantly related to another Dr. Satori, an oncologist who had taken care of Yoshiro's mother long ago, though the two didn't look or sound anything like each other. The oncologist had always treated his patients like children. He took any question as a personal attack, raising his eyebrows and spluttering, "If you don't stop doubting me and do exactly as I say you'll never get well." Dr. Satori the pediatrician, on the other hand, freely shared his knowledge with Yoshiro and Mumei. He never talked down to them, and wasn't at all afraid of questions or even of criticism. Nevertheless, Yoshiro rarely asked him about anything. Seeing the numbers on Mumei's chart, he was certain that only pain and death lurked behind them, so he simply nodded and let it go at that.

The results of children's "monthly look-overs" were copied by hand, then delivered to the Central Division of the New Japan Medical Research Center by a foot messenger. A popular manga entitled *A Message from the Sea Breeze*, about a foot messenger with the legs of a Japanese antelope and a map of every town in the country in his head, inspired lots of children to dream of becoming foot messengers when they grew up, though the general deterioration in physical strength among the young would make that impossible—in the near future, young people would probably all work in offices and physical labor would be left to the elderly.

All original data concerning children's health was recorded by hand, with each doctor hiding his patients' data in a place of his own choosing. There were cartoons in the newspaper showing doctors squirreling files away in dog-houses, or at the bottom of huge cauldrons. Though Yoshiro laughed when he saw them, it would occur to him later that this might be more reality than satire.

Because the data that each clinic delivered to the Medical Research Center were handwritten copies of handwritten originals, any attempt at erasing or tampering with large amounts of data would take an awfully long time. In this sense, the current system was safer than the security systems invented by even the best computer programmers in earlier times.

Now that the adjective *healthy* didn't really fit any child, pediatricians were not only working longer hours, but also had to face the parents' anger and sadness as well as feel pressure from unknown sources whenever they tried to explain the situation to newspapers or other public media. Many suffered from insomnia, or were even driven to suicide until finally the surviving pediatricians formed a labor union, boldly announcing a reduction in their working hours, refusing to submit reports demanded by insurance companies, and cutting all ties with the major pharmaceutical firms.

Mumei liked his pediatrician, so he never minded going for his monthly look-over. Visits to the dentist were as exciting to him as a school excursion—only Yoshiro found them depressing. Mumei loved sitting high up in the chair, talking to the dentist. On a recent visit, the dentist had said, "You mustn't force milk on children who hate the smell. And even if they like it, you shouldn't give them too much."

"Yes, I've heard that," said Yoshiro, while the dentist peered down at Mumei and asked gravely, "Do you like milk?"

Without skipping a beat Mumei replied, "I like worms better." Unable to see the line that connected milk to worms, in his confusion Yoshiro let his eyes wander out the window, yet the dentist didn't seem the least bit perturbed. "I see," he said, "so that means you're a baby bird rather than a calf. While calves drink their mother's milk, baby birds eat the worms their parents bring them. But worms live in the earth, so when the earth is contaminated, the contamination gets concentrated in the worms. That's why birds don't eat many worms these days. Which explains why there are so many worms now that it's easy to catch one. After it rains, you see lots of them squirming around in the middle of the road. You'd better not eat those worms, though—stick to bugs you catch flying through the air."

He sounded so matter-of-fact he might have been explaining how teeth should be brushed. Did knowing Yoshiro was a writer make him want to compete, to send his words flying off somewhere no writer would think to go? Or had Mumei and the dentist already moved on to some future dimension, leaving him far behind?

Many dentists like to show off their speaking skills, probably because the more they talk the more their beautiful teeth are on display. This dentist was about to celebrate his 105th birthday, yet his jaw was still firm, his mouth lined with big, square, gleaming white teeth. Yoshiro was secretly thinking how much he'd like to steal those fine teeth to give to his great-grandson when the dentist opened his mouth and started talking again.

"According to one theory, it's best to get your calcium from the bones of fish and animals. But they have to be from before the earth became irreversibly contaminated. So some people say we should dig way, way down underground to find dinosaur bones. In Hokkaido there are already shops that sell powder from ground Naumann Mammoth bones they've dug up there."

By some strange coincidence the very next day, when he was passing the elementary school, Yoshiro happened to see a poster announcing a lecture on the Naumann Mammoth, to be given by a university professor of paleontology at the Cultural Park, and because lectures were a hobby of his, as soon as he got home he wrote *Naumann Mammoth* on the wall calendar. Mumei stopped in his tracks every time he passed the calendar, blinking furiously, his eyes glued to the words "Naumann Mammoth." To Mumei, the words themselves were an animal that would start moving if only he stared at it long enough.

To break the spell that had nailed Mumei to the floor in front of the calendar, Yoshiro said, "The Naumann Mammoth is a kind of elephant that lived some five hundred thousand years ago. Some professor's going to give a talk about it. Why don't we go hear him?" His face lit up with joy, Mumei thrust both arms above his head, shouting, "Paradise!" as he jumped up in the air. Though astounded at the time, Yoshiro later forgot all about Mumei's amazing leap.

It wasn't just the Naumann Mammoth that cast a spell on Mumei. When he heard or saw the word *heron*, for instance, or *sea turtle*, he became obsessed, unable to take his eyes off the name from which he believed a living creature might emerge.

Encountering a real animal—not just its name—would

have set Mumei's heart on fire, but wild animals had not been seen in Japan for many years. As a student, Yoshiro had traveled to Kyoto through the mountains along the Nakasendo Trail with a German girl from a town called Mettmann. He had been shocked to hear her say, "The only wild animals in Japan are spiders and crows." Now that the country was closed to the outside world, no more visitors came from afar to wake people up with a jab like that. Whenever he thought about animals, Yoshiro remembered the German girl. Her name was Hildegard. She and Yoshiro were the same age. Sometimes he still heard her voice saying, "Hello, Yo-shi-ro?" Even now, when there were no telephones, he would hear an electronic buzz in the air followed by "Hallo," repeated several times, then, "Yo-shi-ro?"—her voice, the way it rose, was still reverberating in his ears. After "Yo" she would take a breath, then sweep upward on "shi," turning up the volume before the final "ro," which cut the name short yet nevertheless sounded like a kind gesture, a welcoming hand stretched out.

Then the conversation would begin, in broken English. Yoshiro would ask a series of simple questions, like "What did you eat today?" or "Where do you buy vegetables?" or "Do little kids in Germany like to play outside?" He was dying to know if the environment in Germany was unchanged, or becoming more contaminated like Japan, and whether her grandchildren and great-grandchildren were healthy. Hildegard would reply, "I'm boiling the green beans I grew in my garden along with some herbs," and at that moment, Yoshiro would be breathing in the steam rising from her saucepan, yet soon the voice on the other end of his imaginary telephone would grow too faint to hear, leaving him unable to tell whether he'd actually heard her voice or just imagined it. Real or not, when he closed his eyes he could see this scene: Hildegard's great-grandchildren running around in the garden, jumping over a pond, standing on tiptoe to pluck apples from a tree, not even bothering to wash them before biting into the sour, worm-eaten fruit with their strong, white teeth. The apple eaten, they'd be wondering whether to go pick wildflowers in the fields or run to the creek to watch the fish.

Yoshiro wanted to visit Hildegard in Germany, just once, but the routes from Japan to all foreign countries had been cut off. Perhaps that was why he no longer felt the roundness of the earth beneath his feet. The round earth he could travel across existed only in his head ... and there was nothing to do but follow that curve in his mind to the other side of the world.

Yoshiro imagined himself packing a small suitcase with clothes and toiletries, then taking the train and bus to Narita Airport. It had been years since he had been to Shinjuku—what was it like now? Billboards, far too gaudy to be overlooking ruins; traffic lights changing regularly from red to green on streets without a single car; automatic doors opening and closing for nonexistent employees, reacting, perhaps, to big branches on the trees that lined the streets, bending down in the wind. In banquet halls, the smell of cigarettes smoked long ago froze in the silver silence; at table after table in the pubs on each floor of multitenant buildings customers called absence caroused, drinking and eating their fill for a flat fee; with no one to borrow money the interest demanded by loan sharks rusted in its tracks; without buyers, mounds of bargain underwear grew damp and fetid; mold formed on handbags displayed in show windows now flooded with rainwater, and rats took leisurely naps inside high-heeled shoes. From sidewalk cracks stalks of shepherd's purse grew straight up, six feet high. Now that human beings had disappeared from this urban center, the cherry trees that had once stood demurely beside sidewalks, slender as brooms, had grown thicker around the trunk, their branches spreading boldly out in all four directions, their luxuriant green afros swaying gently back and forth in the breeze.

Yoshiro imagined himself at Shinjuku Station, boarding a deserted Narita Express for the airport. In fact, no one was riding the Express, the train whose foreign name had once projected the very image of speed, or drinking espresso either. At the airport terminal there was no one at the checkpoint, so no need to show his passport. The TERMINAL sign, written in Chinese characters, had been taken down long ago, and was now propped up against a wall. Climbing the creaky steps of the frozen escalator, he found all the check-in counters abandoned, a huge spider's web covering each one like an umbrella. Looking more closely, he saw that there was a spider about the size of the palm of his hand in each one, calmly waiting for prey. There were colorful stripes on one spider's back; black at the top, red, then yellow. Germany was his destination—that must explain it, he thought. He took a cautious look at the counter next door and saw that its spider had red, white, and blue stripes. There were smaller red spiders here and there in the web too, with white stars on their backs.

Yoshiro didn't know why he was able to picture the airport so clearly. With no effort on his part, these images just came to him, begging to be written into a novel. But it would be dangerous to write about an airport nobody went to anymore. What if the government was keeping it off limits to the public on purpose, because state secrets were hidden there? Sneaking into a forbidden place to dig up forbidden knowledge didn't interest him at all. But even if what he published was only a description of what he had imagined, if his fiction happened to correspond too closely to what the airport was really like he might be arrested for leaking state secrets. Proving in a court of law that it had come from his imagination might be awfully difficult. And would they even give him a trial? Not that he found the idea of going to prison particularly frightening, but wondering how Mumei would survive without him worried him so much that he couldn't bring himself to take many risks.

How many years had it been since the absence of animals other than rental dogs and dead cats had ceased to bother him? Though he had heard something about a "Rabbit Union" formed by people who secretly kept rabbits, since he didn't know anyone who belonged, he couldn't even show Mumei a living rabbit.

"Mumei, are you going to be a zoologist?" he would ask as he watched Mumei totally absorbed in drawing a zebra, copying the picture from his *Illustrated Guide to Animals*. In the old man's dreams, Mumei not only became a professor of zoology, but traveled the world, observing wild animals, writing essays about his travels that would make his name as a writer as well. This dream always softened his face with a smile that never took very long to freeze into a frown.

Yoshiro sat down on the toilet, imagining the colossal rear end of a Naumann Mammoth. Letting his imagination go, he watched Mumei examine the puddle left by the mammoth's footprint through a magnifying glass. Then, he angrily grabbed a handful of toilet paper. Yoshiro kept newspaper clippings he'd softened in his hands in a wooden frame box to use as toilet paper. Like having politics stuck up his ass, he thought, shuddering in disgust, but then again when they touched him, those articles were upside down, turned into mirror writing—a comforting notion after all. For beneath his bottom, the political trends up to now were reversed, moving backwards, in opposition.

Though he had once cut out every newspaper article he found on children's health and carefully filed it away, he had given all that up long ago. He'd never actually reread any of the articles, and the files had just kept growing until they started to take over his bookshelves, making the walls oppressive. "Never throw anything away without a good reason," a rule he had always strictly kept, gradually became, as weeks of living in temporary housing dragged into years, "Throw away anything you haven't needed during the last six months."

There was one more reason why he hadn't hesitated to throw away those old newspaper articles. Information concerning children's health was as capricious as autumn weather, or a man's heart. One article recommended "Early to Rise" as the road to health, but just a few days later the headlines screamed "Kids Who Sleep Late Grow Faster." On the heels of "Snacking Leads to Poor Appetites" would come an essay proclaiming that kids who aren't given sweets whenever they want grow up to be gloomy. "Make Your Children Walk," advised an expert one day, followed almost immediately by a story about a child who was forced to walk until the bones in his knees wore out. Unable to foresee what sort of fate awaited Mumei in the future, Yoshiro kept his eyes open, taking each day as it came, hoping the present wouldn't crumble under his feet.

A cooking pot gleamed arrogantly in the kitchen. It wasn't a particularly high-quality pot, so why did it have to put on such a shine? Glancing at it, Yoshiro took a big kitchen knife and sliced an orange in half. The knife shone, too, but humbly. He had the baker to thank for this kitchen knife that cut so well. He had told Yoshiro about a friend of his who was selling knives at a nearby bookstore the following week. When Yoshiro asked why they were selling kitchen knives at a bookstore, the baker explained that his friend, having also written a best-selling autobiography, would be selling the knives he made at his book signing. He mustn't think the "Tosa-ken" burned into the wooden knife handles meant the dog, the baker had added with a grin. Tosa, apparently, was just the brand name. When Yoshiro arrived at the bookstore there were already about fifty people lined up. He hadn't been this excited waiting in line for a long time. At last, his turn came. He bought a book-and-knife set, and while the baker's friend was signing his book, asked, "Are you touring the entire country?"

"No, this time I'm only going to Hyogo Prefecture and the Far West of Tokyo."

Oh, so people from outside now call this area "the Far West of Tokyo," thought Yoshiro—an odd way to put it, with that same sort of faraway, exotic feel as "the Middle East" or "the Near East," names you never heard anymore.

If the master cutler noticed Yoshiro's reaction to "the Far West of Tokyo," he didn't show it. "Actually, these knives would probably sell better in Tohoku or Hokkaido," he went on. "The economy's booming up there. It's awfully far away, though. Years ago when I used to go to New York to sell my knives it didn't seem far at all—distance is odd that way."

His voice dropped to a raspy whisper on "New York." There was a strange new law against saying the names of foreign cities out loud, and although no one had been prosecuted for breaking it yet, all the same people were very being careful. Nothing is more frightening than a law that has never been enforced. When the authorities want to throw someone in jail, all they have to do is suddenly arrest him for breaking a law that no one has bothered to obey yet.

Though he was glad he had bought the knife, the autobiography was just a typical success story, demanding the reader's tears as a reward for the teller's pains; after slogging through the first half Yoshiro could go no further. Even so, there was one exceptionally vivid passage. It was the part about how the author always got up before sunrise, lit a candle and went into his workshop, still so sleepy he didn't know who he was. Because he was basically a night person it was hard getting up so early, yet the rule that he had to rise before dawn was the only one he never broke. As to its origin—whether it was religious in nature, a tradition among cutlers, or a family custom, passed down through the generations—there was no explanation. But as if to make up for that lack of deeper background information, the dimensions of the candle were meticulously described—it was exactly two inches in diameter and four inches tall.

Wondering how the baker knew this cutler from Tosa, the island of Shikoku, the next time he went to buy bread Yoshiro casually asked, "Did you used to live in Shikoku?"

"I went there in search of the roots of Sanuki bread," the baker replied. Yoshiro was eager to hear more about these travels, but the baker, usually so talkative, turned coldly back to his work.

The knife was a good buy. When he grasped the handle, a second heart began to beat in Yoshiro's hand. Some might say it's silly to put so much energy into cutting up fruit, but Yoshiro had chosen not a fish or a piece of meat but an orange as this blade's first and fiercest adversary. His mission—to seek out the noble drops hidden deep inside the fruit, protected by impenetrable walls of fiber, and deliver them to Mumei—had him trembling. Ah, this tough, unyielding rind, with its strong yet elegant white citrus gloves beneath, surrounding each section with its many juice sacs to hold the precious liquid, all determined not to let a single drop escape. Why must you put so many wrappings in the way, preventing my beloved great-grandson from enjoying the sweetness of your juice!

It wasn't only fruit. Cabbage and burdock root, too, with their barricades of finely woven fiber, seemed to tease, "Just try eating us!" Plants might look placid on the surface, but they refuse to give an inch. And it was this stubbornness he resented. And so his knife headed straight for its target, never hesitating, never stopping, slicing right into it. Not aggressive or pushy, but it kept on cutting, its blade fine and sharp—it didn't waste time on needless anxiety.

"Just wait, Mumei. Great-grandpa will cut through the jungle of vegetable fiber your teeth can't manage, carving out the road to health and life. I will be your teeth. Mumei, absorb the sun into your body. Imagine you're a shark, your mouth full of fine, white teeth, so huge and sharp that whoever sees them runs away in terror. Your saliva is at high tide, wave upon wave filling your mouth, your throat muscles so strong you could swallow the earth. Your gut is an indoor pool, full of gastric juices, and under its glass roof the sun soaks in your gastric pool. Unlike other planets, the earth is blessed with the sun's light every day. Thanks to Lord Apollo, it is full of strange and wonderful forms. Even now, jellyfish, octopi, frilled lizards, crabs, rhinoceroses, human beings, and lots of other creatures live on the earth, changing all the time. Buds sprout from an embryo, which opens in the shape of a heart, tadpoles like little musical notes turn into frogs like the round wooden drums you see in temples, caterpillars become butterflies, wrinkly newborns age into wrinkled old men. In the past ten years or so, lots of species have gone extinct, but the earth is still warm, and bright."

Silently chanting phrases he would have been embarrassed to say out loud, Yoshiro fiddled with the knife in his hand until he found just the right grip. He would slice this orange in two and squeeze the juice out for Mumei. Peeling an orange and then cutting it up into little pieces took so much time that the boy had often been late for school. But surely he'd manage to drink a glass of juice in about fifteen minutes. That said, drinking was no easy task for Mumei. His eyes circling in their sockets with the effort, he would struggle to keep his Adam's apple pumping up and down like an elevator, trying to force the liquid down. Sometimes it would come back up, burning his throat. Or on its way down it would enter his bronchial tubes instead, bringing on a coughing fit. Once he started coughing it was hard to get him to stop.

"Mumei, are you all right? Does it hurt? Can you breathe?" Yoshiro would say, his eyes filling with tears as he patted the boy lightly on the back, or held his head in his arms, pressing it to his chest. Yet despite the appearance of suffering, Mumei himself would be strangely calm. As if resigning himself to a storm at sea, he'd simply wait for the coughing fit to pass.

When the coughing stopped, Mumei would go back to drinking his juice as if nothing had happened. Looking up at Yoshiro, he would ask in surprise, "Great-grandpa, are you all right?" He didn't seem to know what "suffering" meant; he simply coughed when food wouldn't go down, or vomited it back up. Of course he felt pain, but it was pure pain, unaccompanied by any "Why am I the only one who has to suffer like this?" sort of lamentations that Yoshiro knew so well. Perhaps this acceptance was a treasure given to the youngest generation. Mumei didn't know how to feel sorry for himself.

When Yoshiro was a child, his mother babied him whenever he caught cold or ran a fever. Wallowing in self-pity had felt sweet, warm, and deliciously sad. As an adult he knew that, although he had to go to work no matter how much he hated it, illness would give him a bona fide excuse for staying at home, spending the whole day in bed reading or just thinking. It was easy to catch the flu. All he had to do was make sure he didn't get enough sleep. And even after he recovered, he always managed to get sick again a few months later. Finally, he realized that his true purpose was not to come down with some illness, but to quit his job.

Fortunately, Mumei had never seen adults clinging to illness in this unseemly way. And if he kept on in this way, he would be free until he died, never feeling sorry for himself or using his weakness to ingratiate himself with the people around him.

For about ninety percent of children these days fever was a constant companion. Mumei was always slightly feverish. As checking the thermometer daily only made the adults nervous, a flier came from school instructing them not to. If told they had a fever, kids would start to feel dull and lethargic. And if they were kept home every time their temperature was above normal, some would hardly go to school at all. Besides, since every school had a qualified doctor on duty, it was really best for them to come to school when they were sick. "Because the purpose of fever is to kill germs, children shouldn't be given medicine to bring down a fever" had been standard medical advice for ages, but only recently had doctors begun to tell parents "Never take your child's temperature."

Yoshiro and Mumei buried their thermometer at the Thingamabob Cemetery, a public graveyard where anyone could pay their last respects to something they wanted to part with. Some of the buried objects, still longing for the world above, were apparently trying to return to it; from the earth, disturbed by the rain that day, part of a white headband with a red Rising Sun in the center peeked out, fluttering in the wind. Yoshiro imagined its former owner as either a high school student who was done with his university entrance exams, or a youth who had graduated from some right-wing gang. The leg of an upside-down teddy bear stuck out of the ground. The bear probably wanted to get out, too. Mumei imagined all the various things buried here: broken garden shears, split into two tadpoles; worn-out shoes with paper-thin soles; a toy drum with a broken head; the wedding ring of a couple now divorced; a fountain pen with a bent tip; a map of the world. Yoshiro had once buried the manuscript of a novel he was working on here. He'd thought of burning it in the garden, but submitting it to the flames had seemed so cruel he couldn't bring himself to strike a match. Everyone has reasons for burning some bits of trash but not others. *Ken-to-shi, Emissary to China*, he'd called it, his first and only historical novel: he was already well into it when he realized he'd included the names of far too many foreign countries. Place names spread throughout the novel like blood vessels, dividing into ever smaller branches, then setting down roots, making it impossible to eliminate them from the text. He'd had to get rid of the manuscript for his own protection, and since burning it was too painful, he had buried it.

*

As white ceramic blades work their way in, orange liquid flows out. This was how Yoshiro wanted to live: shedding not blood, not tears, but a steady stream of juice. Taking in the warmth and cheer possessed only by the orange, with its combination of tart and sweet that firms up flaccid flesh, feeling the sun in his gut.

After carefully pouring the freshly squeezed juice, he cupped the empty halves of orange peel in his right hand, putting all his strength into squeezing out the last drops.

"Why don't you drink any, Great-grandpa?" asked Mumei.

"I could only get one orange this time," answered Yoshiro, "and besides, you kids have to live a long time. So you always come first."

"Grown-ups can live if children die," Mumei replied in a singsong voice, "but if grown-ups die, children can't live." Yoshiro fell silent.

Whenever he tried to imagine the years Mumei would have to go on living after his own death, Yoshiro ran straight into a wall. For an old man like Yoshiro, time after death no longer existed. The aged could not die; along with the gift of everlasting life, they were burdened with terrible task of watching their great-grandchildren die.

Mumei's generation might create a new civilization— which they would leave to their elders. From birth Mumei had seemed to possess a mysterious kind of wisdom, a depth that Yoshiro had never seen in a child before.

When his daughter Amana had been Mumei's age, she would eat a whole box of cookies or chocolates if the con-

tainer where they were kept wasn't locked, but any attempt
to scold her always ended in a fight.

"You mustn't eat so many sweets all at once."

"Why?"

"Because it's bad for you."

"Why?"

"Because you'll be too full to eat dinner and wind up un-
dernourished."

"So I can have all the sweets I want as long as I eat dinner,
right?"

"Of course not."

"Why?"

Exhausted from this endless barrage, Yoshiro would end
up screaming, "When I say no it means no!" Not that he
wanted to be an overbearing father; it was just that as soon
as his daughter started talking her mouth emitted a steady
stream of "I want," "I want," "I WANT!"

In a fair, democratic fight, he was sure to lose. The purpose
of authoritarianism, it seemed to him, was to protect these
foolish, vulnerable creatures called parents.

There was no limit to his daughter's desires. She would
keep eating sweets until she made herself sick, or refuse to
budge from a toy store until he bought her what she wanted.
When she resorted to grabbing sweets or toys away from
other children, Yoshiro had to step in. The child's role was
to unleash desire, the parent's to stop her. As a little girl, she
had put up with these parental restrictions. But as her voice
grew louder, her vocabulary increased daily, along with her
skill at making excuses for herself. For every harsh word he
spoke she would lob back ten at him, sharp as arrows. Their

tips hurt, sometimes even drawing blood, making Yoshiro hope she would gorge herself on ice cream until her belly ached, but all the same he never lost his conviction that he had worthwhile lessons to teach her. With Mumei, things were completely different: the boy never ate too much, or put anything in his mouth that didn't belong there, yet Yoshiro had not a single thing to teach him about life. This made him feel so pathetic that he could only close his eyes and press clenched fists into them in a gesture of utter despair.

From the time his grandson Tomo was still small enough to lift up, Yoshiro had looked forward to the day when he would teach him how to be a safe driver. Though writers are generally considered to be imaginative, Yoshiro had never imagined that cars would one day disappear. As the boy hadn't cared much for studying, Yoshiro had given him a bankbook for an account with enough money to pay for three years' tuition at an occupational training school, but his grandson had secretly closed the account, stuffed all the money into a sports bag, and stole away with it like a thief in the night. When documents came from the bank showing that the account had been dissolved, Yoshiro's gut seethed, steam rising from it until a month later when all the major banks started failing one after another, causing customers to lose all their savings, leaving them with nothing to cling to but rumors about how they would get their money back someday. People stormed the banks, nostrils flared, faces red with anger, to be met by men in suits lined up in front of each branch, sweat pouring off their foreheads as they earnestly spewed out apology after apology. Cursed and screamed at, the men bore up under scorching heat during the day, followed by evening showers that drenched them and swarms of mosquitos that bit them as they continued to bow and apologize until finally the customers folded up their anger for the time being and went home. Then a newspaper article revealed that the men in suits were actually "Sorry-men," hired for an hourly wage to stand in front of branch offices to bow and scrape. Which meant that Tomo, who had never trusted institutions like banks, turned out to have a more practical grasp of economics than Yoshiro, who believed that a savings account could provide security for life. And the same was true of occupational training schools. Several years after that, Yoshiro saw an article in the newspaper by a scholar of contemporary culture who wrote:

"Schools claiming to prepare students to pass certification exams take in a steady income from monthly tuition despite the fact that their graduates, even if they pass the exams, often can't find jobs, or at best, end up settling for very low wages. New occupations with fancy-sounding names must be viewed with particular suspicion. Believing that acceptance at a training school means that their child's special talent has been recognized, parents are glad to pay the tuition. The more expensive the happier they are to pay, for paying more seems to increase their own value. Both parents and child want to show off, afraid of what their neighbors will think if it looks like they aren't doing anything. Recently, more and more dishonest occupational training schools are using this sort of psychology to their own advantage. Have we all forgotten that occupational training was meant to be free and open to everyone?" Long before this highly respected scholar gave the problem his serious attention, a certain juvenile delinquent who trusted neither bank accounts nor occupational training schools had made his escape.

Yoshiro had to admit it: what he had taught his grandson had been all wrong. He remembered telling the boy, "You can't go wrong with real estate. Get yourself some land in a prime location in the middle of Tokyo and you're fixed for life—its value will never go down," but now that all of Tokyo's twenty-three wards, including prime locations, were designated an "exposure to multiple health hazards from prolonged habitation" area, neither its houses nor its land had any monetary value. This designation was supposed to mean that although when measured separately, neither drinking water, air, light, nor food was over the danger line, there was a high probability of multiple pernicious influences from lengthy exposure to the environment as a whole. Whereas individual factors can be measured specifically, human beings live in the general. Even though the twenty-three wards had never actually been classified as dangerous, more and more people wanted to leave, and since they didn't want to go too far, and because living near the sea was particularly dangerous, they began migrating toward the mountainous region from Okutama to Nagano Prefecture. Yoshiro's wife Marika wasn't the only one to abandon the house and land she had inherited in central Tokyo because she couldn't find a buyer.

Assuming he had knowledge and wealth to leave to his descendants was mere arrogance, Yoshiro now realized. This life with his great-grandson was about all he could manage. And for that he needed to be flexible, in mind and body, with the courage to doubt what he had believed for over a century. Sloughing off his pride like an old jacket, he'd have to go around in his shirtsleeves. If he was cold, rather than buying a new jacket it would be better to think of ways to grow a thick coat of fur like a bear's. He was not really an "old man," but a man who, after living for a century, had become a new species of human being, he thought, clenching his fists again and again.

With a thud the newspaper hit the doorstep. As he did every morning Yoshiro ran outside, but no matter how fast he was the woman who delivered his paper would already be so far away that her back was no bigger than his middle finger. It was a thin back, with sloping shoulders and a long slender neck topped with hair in a bun as round as a ball. As Yoshiro watched her firm, round hips and muscular calves recede into the distance, he called loudly after her, "Thanks for the paper!" As she never reacted, he didn't know whether she heard him or not.

On his front doorstep, Yoshiro unrolled the paper. He hadn't paid much attention to the newspaper as a young man, but ever since this media had been revived after its disappearance, reading it carefully all the way through had become a daily ritual. As he let his eyes fly low over the Politics section, words such as *regulation, standard, adaptation, policy, investigation,* and *caution* stuck out like stalks in a flattened field. Actually reading this section was like slogging through a swamp. He mustn't spend his mornings this way; first, he had to get Mumei off to school. The word *school* still carried a faint whiff of hope.

Leaving the newspaper in the foyer he went back to the kitchen, where he handed Mumei his orange juice in a bamboo cup with a narrow drinking spout.

After taking a swallow, Mumei asked, "We get oranges from Okinawa, don't we?"

"That's right."

"Do oranges grow further south than Okinawa?"

Yoshiro swallowed hard. "You know, I'm not really sure."

"Why not?"

"Because Japan is closed to the outside world."

"Why is it closed?"

"Every country has serious problems, so to keep those problems from spreading all around the world, they decided that each country should solve its own problems by itself. Remember when I took you to the Showa-Heisei Museum? All the rooms were separated by steel doors, so if a fire starts in one room it can't spread to the next one."

"It is better that way?"

"I don't know if it's better or not. But at least this way there's less danger of Japanese companies making money off the poor people living in other countries. And there are probably fewer chances for foreign companies to make money from the crisis we're having here in Japan, too."

Mumei looked puzzled, as if maybe he sort of understood, but not quite. Yoshiro was always careful not to tell him that he didn't really support Japan's isolation policy.

Although no one openly discussed the isolation policy, there was lots of griping about fruit. Ever since Japan had stopped importing food from abroad, all the oranges, pineapples and bananas came from Okinawa. Lots of mandarin oranges were apparently being harvested on the island of Shikoku, but they hardly ever made it to Tokyo. Shikoku had adopted a policy of keeping its fruit for its own people, generating income from its patents on recipes for Sanuki noodles and German bread instead.

One day when Yoshiro saw mandarin oranges on sale at the bakery, he immediately bought two. Both were labeled "Made in Shikoku." The baker definitely had deep island connections. Yoshiro had planned to keep the oranges for Saturday, when he and Mumei would be able to take their time eating them, but before Saturday came there was a new holiday he'd forgotten all about. Nowadays there were so many holidays that Yoshiro couldn't keep track of them all. He was always checking the calendar, trying to remember, but they never seemed to take root in his brain.

Unlike the old holiday to commemorate the Emperor's birthday, the new ones were perfectly democratic, their names and dates decided by popular elections. First, ideas were solicited from the public. Various suggestions were offered. "Ocean Day" provides ample opportunities to think about pollution of the seas, one group said, but after decades of pouring the filthy runoff from factories into the rivers, shouldn't we also honor them with a "River Day"? Or, since we have a "Green Day," why not a "Red Day" to go with it? As "Culture Day" was too abstract to have much meaning, the people overwhelmingly voted to make it more specific by adding "Book Day," "Song Day," "Musical Instrument Day," "Picture Day" and "Architecture Day." The names of some of the older holidays were changed: "Respect for the Aged Day" became "Encouragement for the Aged Day," while "Children's Day" was now "Apologize to the Children Day"; "Sports Day" was changed to "Body Day" to avoid upsetting children who were not growing up big and strong; so as not to hurt the feelings of young people who wanted to work but simply weren't strong enough, "Labor Day" became "Being Alive Is Enough Day." Increasing the number of public holidays wasn't the only thing on people's minds. The stream of voices calling for the abolition of "National Founding Day" grew into a deluge, washing this holiday away so completely it was never heard from again. The main objection was that a splendid country like Japan could not possibly have been founded in a single day. Other new holidays included "Pillow Day," to encourage couples to have sex, which was almost unheard of these days; "Extinct Species Day," when people lit sticks of incense in memory of birds and animals that had vanished from the earth; "Off-line Day," to commemorate the day the Internet had died ("off-line" being written with Chinese characters meaning 'Honorable-Woman-Naked-Obscenity'); and "Bone Day," for seriously considering the importance of calcium.

The mandarin orange put Mumei in such a good mood that he immediately started playing with it, poking a section with his finger, which was about as soft as the orange. On the verge of scolding, "Don't play with your food," Yoshiro stuffed some orange into his mouth to stop himself. Playing with food was fine. He might even discover a new way of eating it. Play, play, play with your food! If Mumei were to ask him, "How do you eat a mandarin orange?" he would tell him to figure it out for himself. Any way would be fine with Great-grandpa. Think of a way as you play. But in the end, Mumei never asked. Yoshiro's generation were brought up believing that there was a proper way to eat fruit: *this* was the way you peeled an orange; you used *this* sort of spoon to scoop out grapefruit sections. They believed that by standardizing the eating process into a ritual, they could soothe their cells into ignoring the sourness of the fruit, which actually warned of danger. Mumei's generation could never be deceived by such a silly trick, originally meant to fool children. No matter how they ate fruit, alarms went off throughout their bodies. When Mumei ate kiwi fruit he had trouble breathing; lemon juice paralyzed his tongue. And it wasn't just fruit. Spinach gave him heartburn, while shiitake mushrooms made him dizzy. Mumei never forgot for an instant that food was dangerous.

"Lemon is so sour it makes you see blue."

This is what Mumei said the first time he ate a lemon snow cone. Ever since, whenever Yoshiro saw a lemon, it seemed to him that blue was mixed in with the yellow—and that made him feel that for just a moment he had touched the raw, spinning earth.

Searching with bloodshot eyes for fruit for their great-grandchildren, old people wandered like ghosts from market to market. Long ago, only the prices of books and magazines had been fixed, but now the cost of fruit and some vegetables was the same all over Japan; regardless of whether there was a surplus or a shortage of oranges, the price of one was set at 10,000 yen. Without inflation, there probably wouldn't have been so many zeros attached to the price of a single piece of fruit.

Due to the violent, capricious personality the climate had developed on the main island of Honshu, farming was becoming more and more difficult. The northern Tohoku region was better off, taking in a good income from a nutritious new strain they called "New Species Multigrain," in addition to more traditional crops like rice and wheat, which they also exported, although in somewhat small amounts. On Honshu, the area from Ibaraki Prefecture to Kyoto was most seriously affected by climate change. In some years fine snow fell in August, while in February, hot dry winds dumped mounds of sand. Eyes red despite the eyewash they'd used, men would creep sideways along the edge of the sidewalk like crabs, trying to stay out of the harsh, desert winds sweeping down the middle of the street. Women in sunglasses with their hair hidden beneath scarves—pacing back and forth as if they were on a movie set where the shoot was going badly—were actually fighting their anxiety about the weather. During the summer, when it didn't rain for three months, all the vegetation would turn dusty yellow until suddenly tropical low pressure would bring on a squall that flooded the subway stations.

Driven by the cycles of droughts following tropical storms, many people moved from Honshu to Okinawa. There were other areas where agriculture was booming— Hokkaido came to mind, but unlike Okinawa, it had adopted an anti-immigration policy so as not to upset the balance between people and nature. Although the population of Hokkaido had long been considered too small for such a large expanse of land, when an expert in population issues from Asahikawa concluded that the current population was actually ideally suited to the land area, the local government decided not to increase the population. No one from another area or prefecture could take up residence without permission, which was never granted without a very special reason.

Although Okinawa basically placed no restrictions on immigration from Honshu, they were afraid of an explosion in the population of single male laborers. To prevent this, it was decided that people who wanted to work on farms in Okinawa had to apply as married couples. Single women could apply as well as same-sex couples, both male and female, but applications from single men were not accepted. Exceptions were made for single women who had a sex change operation after they became residents; they were allowed to stay as single men. Only prospective immigrants with jobs lined up were allowed to apply, and since there were very few jobs outside of agriculture, it was safe to say that without a farm to employ them, people from Honshu wouldn't receive permission to immigrate.

Due to a shortage of day care centers and after-school programs, couples with children under the age of twelve were not accepted, although exceptions were made for couples who left their children with relatives or foster families and came by themselves. Because the local government didn't want immigrants to have children once they'd moved to Okinawa, women over the age of fifty-five and men who had had vasectomies were preferred. There was an article in the newspaper about a woman who drew wrinkles on her face and dyed her hair white in an attempt to hide her youth, but acting older than your real age is actually quite difficult. Suspicion fell on her when people realized she couldn't tell the ON and OFF switches on old farm machinery apart, which meant she must have been younger than she looked. The ability to understand even a little English was evidence of old age. As studying English was now prohibited, young people didn't know even simple words like *on* and *off*. It was okay to study other languages such as Tagalog, German, Swahili, or Czechoslovakian, though it was so hard to find teachers, textbooks, or even people who had studied these languages that not many people even wanted to try. Singing songs in foreign languages in public places for over forty seconds was strictly prohibited. Nor could novels translated from foreign languages be published.

Yoshiro's only daughter Amana had eagerly immigrated to Okinawa with her husband, their youthful sixtyish muscles clad in blue cotton work clothes they'd had made by special order. Believing that work clothes should match the wearer's personality, they never even considered buying ready-made outfits. Amana's hair, luxuriant enough to cover the whole bed when she was lying down, was bundled up under a straw hat while she was working; the hat, too, she'd had made specially, according to her own design.

Yoshiro hadn't seen his daughter in a long time. He sometimes read in the newspaper about how life in Okinawa was more prosperous than anyone in Tokyo could imagine. Fruits and vegetables were practically free. Yet because individuals were prohibited from shipping agricultural products to places outside of Okinawa, immigrants couldn't send food to their families in Tokyo.

Food from farms on each of Okinawa's islands was carried to local ports by "horse and wagon," where it was loaded onto ships owned by a transportation company in Kyushu, and then brought to the major port of Shin-makurazaki. Despite the nomenclature "horse and wagon," there were no horses to pull wagons. Satirical cartoons in the newspaper showed dogs, foxes, and wild boars pulling wagons full of fruit, which may have been reality rather than satire.

A number of transit companies in Kyushu had cargo ships covered with solar panels that looked like huge mushrooms, the largest being Risshin Marine Transport, whose ships carried most of the Okinawan produce to areas all over Japan. Well, not quite all over—most of the expensive fruit was bound for Tohoku and Hokkaido, in the north, while hardly any of it reached Tokyo. In exchange, tons of rice and salmon were shipped from the north to Okinawa. In this age when paper money, stocks, and interest had lost their luster, people who could barter had top priority. Salmon had been thought extinct for a time, until a strange new breed with stars all over its body was discovered. It was said that eating it could damage the liver, but even so, people loved that old-style salmon flavor.

Unlike the twenty-three wards of central Tokyo, which were virtually deserted, the Tama area in the surrounding mountains was still heavily populated, though with no industry of its own, it was growing poorer by the day. Yoshiro was old enough to remember the funeral of the last living politician to be driven from his post for saying things like, "If Tokyo fails the whole country will go down with it. We must save Tokyo even if it means sacrificing all the outlying prefectures!" While he certainly didn't approve of the egotism of Edo—now called Edonism—just saying "Tokyo" aloud still excited him somehow, bringing back an enthusiasm for the city he couldn't let go of, making the thought of Tokyo disappearing altogether so unbearable he thought he'd just as soon vanish along with it.

There were plans to revitalize Tokyo by developing products peculiar to the city. When he read in the newspaper about a project to resurrect Tokyo's preindustrial charm by selling new products with the brand name "Edo," he thought he'd like to take part.

Soybeans and buckwheat were still grown in the "Far West" of Tokyo, along with a new strain of wheat, but not enough was produced to export to other regions, and besides, these were crops that could be grown elsewhere. Long ago, the words "something new from Tokyo" brought to mind a plug attached to a long tail called a cord, but things like that didn't sell anymore. Electrical appliances had met with disapproval ever since electric current was discovered to cause nervous disorders, numbness in the extremities, and insomnia—a condition generally known as bzzt-bzzt syndrome. Newspapers carried reports of chronic insomniacs who slept soundly at camping grounds in the mountains where there was no electricity. A popular writer published an essay on how the sound of a vacuum cleaner drove all thoughts of the novel he was writing out of his mind. Though this essay probably wasn't the only cause, around the time it was published, resentment against vacuum cleaners began to spread throughout society. To Yoshiro, who had always thought that the vacuum cleaner's metallic groan must come through a tunnel from the depths of hell, this was a welcome trend. As temporary prefab houses had been specially built so that they could easily be kept clean with a broom and mop-up rags, their inhabitants were the first to stop using vacuum cleaners. Washing machines disappeared as well. Residents of temporary housing blocks were also the first to start washing cotton underwear by hand and hanging it out to dry. The cleaners came for the rest of their clothes, which they washed and brought back (*cleaning* being a foreign word, dry cleaners had almost gone extinct until someone got the idea of writing it in Chinese characters meaning "chestnut-person-tool"). Cleaners were popular not only because paying them was cheaper than buying a new washing machine every three years, but also because of an odd new theory that had taken a curious hold on people's imaginations: Listening to clothes slosh around in a washing machine makes your thoughts dry up. There was even an elementary school that claimed to have conducted an experiment proving that if all electrical appliances were turned off while children were doing their homework, their grades improved dramatically.

Just the sound of the washing machine had been enough to depress Yoshiro when he was young; at least he didn't have that to worry about anymore. Since watching television led to weight gain, many dieters threw theirs away. Air conditioners had gone out of fashion more than a generation ago. The only appliance left was the refrigerator, though the ones now in use didn't have cords. The most popular model, the "Arctic Star," ran on solar energy.

The entire country looked up to the inhabitants of Tokyo's temporary housing blocks, the very first to give up their electrical appliances, as a model of the most advanced lifestyle.

But "nonuse of existing machines" was difficult to market as a new product. To make "revitalization" a success, you really needed something people could see.

How to get back Tokyo's thunder? Could "thunder crackers" be the answer? After all, they were a traditional Edo specialty, named after the Thunder Gate of a temple in the oldest part of the city. Unfortunately, thunder produces electricity. Ironically, the search for something to revitalize Tokyo in the old Edo culture, before electricity was even invented, led straight back to electricity.

A vegetable that could only be grown in Tokyo would certainly be a Tokyo specialty, but no such plant seemed to exist. They'd have to use their heads, or rather, since no other body part seemed likely to find an answer, they hoped their heads were up to the job. How about capitalizing on some crop that could be grown in other areas but that no one had paid much attention to? A love of novelty was said to be the essence of the Edo spirit, but now that they couldn't market new things imported from abroad, some people suggested a turn toward old, forgotten things that could be brought back to life in the present age.

It was this trend that brought a man who came to be known as Dr. Myoga into the spotlight for a time. He hit on a passage from a novel written in the late 1920s: "Myoga grows well behind the outhouse." Huge public outhouses were something one often saw in Tokyo but only rarely in outlying prefectures. Dr. Myoga bought up the dark, wet patches of land behind every public outhouse he could find, and on each one set up a glass box over six feet high, partitioned off inside with shelves about a foot wide where, using artificial dirt mixed with minerals, he grew the herb called myoga. Dr. Myoga never told anyone why this herb grew so well behind outhouses. Instead, he often spoke of how Buddhist priests in training for a life of asceticism expressly avoided it—this in itself, he claimed, was evidence of how stimulating it was, even though it didn't look very nutritious. Although people had always believed that children wouldn't care for the taste, if you gave it to kids nowadays they would gobble it up like ice cream. This, asserted Dr. Myoga, was because it was full of a certain nutrient, unknown until now, that revitalized children from within.

Yoshiro once bought some myoga at the market to give to Mumei. When he smelled it his eyes narrowed in a dreamy smile—it clearly agreed with him. Yet that was the only time Yoshiro saw myoga at the market, and before long the name "Dr. Myoga" was overgrown with forget-me-knotweeds.

Another Tokyo vegetable that gained popularity for a time was nettles. Due to a longstanding prejudice created by the proverb "Some prefer nettles," not even the most eccentric farmers in other prefectures wanted to grow them. Capitalizing on this lack of popularity, a certain company got the idea of marketing nettles as a Tokyo specialty. They even put up posters showing the mayor of Tokyo happily munching away at nettle salad, though it was whispered in some quarters that this may have actually hurt the vegetable's reputation. A new tongue twister, "How many nettles were netted in Nettie's knitted net?" did manage to twist a number of tongues, but unfortunately, the nettles themselves rarely made it as far as anyone's tongue. One day, while Yoshiro was standing in front of a vegetable stand, unable to take his eyes off of a bunch of some deep green vegetable he had never seen before, the shop owner, seizing on this opportunity, spoke to him.

"Those are the nettles everyone's talking about. Why not buy a bunch, to cheer Tokyo on?"

Yoshiro should have been suspicious when this shop owner, whose usual pitch was "This tastes really good" suddenly asked him to "cheer Tokyo on," as if they were at a baseball tournament. He ended up buying a bunch, which he pounded in an earthenware mortar, then mixed with vinegar. Nettles are supposed to go well with sweetfish, but as he didn't want to give Mumei any kind of fish, which were all said to be highly contaminated, he tried boiling the nettles along with some tofu.

"Gee, I'm sorry. This tastes awful." Unable to bear the itch of regret, he scratched his head as he apologized to Mumei, but the boy gazed up at him with a puzzled look and said, "Whether food tastes good or not doesn't really bother me."

The boy had shown him his own shallowness when he had least expected it, making Yoshiro so ashamed he could hardly breathe. Criticism from young people tends to upset the elderly, but Yoshiro wasn't the slightest bit angry with Mumei. What really pained him was the way his generation was always hurting young people without realizing it. Adults arrogantly talked about whether food tasted good or not, as if a gourmet sensibility put you in a superior class of people, forgetting that everyone was already sunk to the waist in a swamp of problems—how must they look to these children? Poison often had no taste at all, so no matter how finely honed your palate, your taste buds weren't going to save your life.

People in Okinawa probably would have laughed at the efforts of Tokyoites to grow myoga or nettles and market them as high-class produce, had they known about them. Yoshiro wrote his daughter Amana a postcard, telling her all about the nettles project, including his own embarrassment at having fallen for it, but she never responded. Perhaps she had never even heard of nettles.

The character for "nettles," 蕁 with all its diagonal slashes, brought the sheer joy of writing back to Yoshiro. He always wrote it slowly, like a young cat scratching the bark of a tree diagonally with its claws.

Yoshiro liked writing picture postcards. Though it seemed strange to be sending postcards to a family member when he wasn't traveling, a page of stationary had so much more space than he had news that whenever he tried writing a letter he ended up not writing anything at all. There was so little space on a postcard that from the first stroke of his pen he could already imagine the period at the end. Being able to see the end of anything gave him a tremendous sense of relief. As a child he had assumed the goal of medicine was to keep bodies alive forever; he had never considered the pain of not being able to die.

Though oranges were sold at a fixed price, postage stamps were not. In fact, costs varied wildly, from the very expensive snow grouse stamp to the one with a photo of the National Diet Building, so cheap it was almost free. Occasionally the post office sold stamps in bulk, one thousand at a bargain price, though Yoshiro never bought them as these sales brought home to him the painful reality that even after writing a thousand more postcards he wouldn't die.

"Perfect postcard weather," he thought, making up his mind to stop in at the postcard shop on his way home from shopping to buy his usual ten. Now that anyone could go into business anytime to sell anything they liked, there were lots of stores that looked like the dinky little stalls students used to set up at school festivals. This postcard shop was no exception; the owner hadn't even bothered to straighten the crooked handmade sign above the entrance. Thinking her homemade postcards weren't quite enough to make a go of it, perhaps, she also stocked a small supply of unusual umbrellas and stationery goods. That day, Yoshiro bought an umbrella that blocked the sunlight despite being transparent. There were also pencils that chirped like birds, origami paper that crinkled into the shape of a pair of mandarin ducks when sprinkled with water, and erasers the size of real lemons, all of which Mumei would probably find irresistible, which was why Yoshiro usually came here by himself.

Pressed flowers had been the proprietor's hobby ever since she'd been at junior high school with Amana. She could form friendships with violets, wave to Chinese plantain grass as she walked by, bow in greeting to shepherd's purse, and write love letters to cosmos, yet still spend every Sunday pulling plants up by the root, then squashing them into the two-dimensional version of nature she sold on her postcards. Most of the plants she used were common weeds, though perhaps *weed* wasn't the right word for plants she went to the trouble of cultivating in her garden, using artificial dirt. When Yoshiro asked why she bothered to plant weeds, she replied, "Because we need more of them. They're about to go extinct, you know. So are mixed-breed dogs, for that matter."

Now that she mentioned it, all the dogs at the Rent-a-Dog store were purebred, and you didn't see dogs anywhere else.

Whenever he came to buy postcards, Yoshiro looked forward to leaning against the pillar by the checkout counter, talking to this woman about his daughter.

"How is Amana-chan getting along? Is she well?"

"I haven't heard anything about her being ill."

"Growing oranges is hard work, isn't it?"

"She seems to be strong enough for it."

"She got plenty of exercise in high school, in the Portable Shrine Club."

"You did track and field, didn't you?"

"Sprinting doesn't do me any good now. No use going hunting, either, when there're no animals out in the fields," she said, brandishing her pencil like a spear, then lifting one knee all the way up to her chest. This pressed-flower artist was young elderly, still in her seventies, girlish enough to burst into giggles at the slightest thing.

"What did Amana-chan have to say in her last letter?"

"Something about seeing a new kind of red pineapple for the first time."

"I envy them down there in Okinawa," she sighed as she handed him his ten postcards, packed neatly into a small envelope made of plant fiber. Hoping to continue the conversation about his daughter, Yoshiro casually added a bit of information he thought might interest her.

"Seems the people in Okinawa call it Ryukyu now."

"Ryukyu? That's a nice name. But they aren't starting an independence movement or anything, are they?"

"I don't think so. If Okinawa became a foreign country

they wouldn't be able to export fruit to Japan, or take in immigrant laborers either, because of the isolation policy."

"That's a relief. It would be awful if we could never see Amana-chan again."

Yoshiro remembered that Hildegard had a Japanese friend named Tsuyukusa. Though he had never met her, Hildegard had told him so much about her that Yoshiro felt as if Tsuyukusa had once been a close friend, sometime long ago. She had gone to the German city of Krefeld, where she still lived, as a young woman, to study the violin. There she had married an Iranian man she met at a concert, and Yoshiro remembered hearing about how after their twins were born, they would come back to Japan to see her parents, Tsuyukusa and her husband each holding one child on their laps in the plane. They used to fly to Japan every year around New Years—how long had it been since they couldn't do that anymore? How must Tsuyukusa feel, knowing she would never be able to return to Japan?

Though far away, Okinawa was still part of Japan, so he could go there if he made the effort. Yet as the thought of actually making the trip left him feeling dull and tired, he always ended up deciding to save all his strength for Mumei.

As a student, he had been friends with a cool young guy who traveled all around South America and Africa with only an uncool sports bag for luggage. When he asked him why he hadn't bought a backpack, his friend had told him that backpacks screamed "Traveler!" so loud it was embarrassing. How cool it would be to set off abroad with just an ordinary sports bag, in old tennis shoes worn down at the heel, as if you were on your way home from the gym. Without announcing "Headed for Foreign Parts." That way you might be inconspicuous enough to slip away without getting arrested.

"A lot of the postcards Amana sends me are written in invisible ink," said Yoshiro as if grasping at a cotton bud that happened to float by, to revive the conversation.

"That's really neat. Okinawans are so lucky to have enough spare fruit to be able to use it for things like that. Does she use lemon juice?"

"Not sure, but I'll ask her. I can still remember discovering invisible ink, how much fun we kids used to have. We formed a secret society—used to bring home top secret documents we got from the others to read. We'd hold them up to the fire on the stove when nobody was looking."

"We used to do that, too. One time my parents scolded me for lighting a candle. What if there's an earthquake, they said."

"How does invisible ink work, exactly?"

"Well, when paper absorbs something sour, like lemon juice, it burns more easily, so when you hold it up to the fire, the letters written in lemon juice turn brown first."

"I see. The juice seeps into the paper like a watercolor, so there's lots of different shades. Some parts are yellow, others brown. Pretty, don't you think?"

"Yeah, the blotches look kind of like a landscape."

"All the postcards Amana sends look like water scenes at first, but if you look carefully you can see the water's burning—there are still tiny flames on it. Kind of scary."

"Water that burns?"

"If enough oil flows into the ocean, it'll burn, won't it?"

"Don't scare me! Amana has a pretty easy life down there, doesn't she?"

"Probably so."

"They have more fruit than they can eat, don't they?"

"That's practically all she writes about. It isn't so interesting, reading about the latest red pineapple, or square pineapple, since they're not going to be shipped here anyway, but actually, I'm getting a little worried. It's strange, her writing about fruit and nothing else. A while ago I might have suspected she'd been brainwashed ..."

The two fell silent, both thinking roughly the same thing. Since orchards are actually factories that produce fruit, working in one all day, cut off from the outside world, might be pretty miserable. The word *orchard* brings a paradise to mind, which makes people envious. They imagine workers walking in the mountains looking for wild mushrooms, discovering miniature farms made of moss on the forest floor on the way as they breathe in moist air wafting through the ferns, reading the hoofprints of deer, or picking out the songs of various birds—playing, really, in nature. That's not what Amana was doing, though—she was working from morning to night in a fruit factory called an orchard. In the city there are art exhibitions, concerts, or lectures on the weekends, as well as other pleasures such as meeting new people, or just walking through the streets, discovering some shop you hadn't noticed before. Though Tokyo was now impoverished, new shops still bubbled up from the depths to open up like flowers; just sitting on a park bench, you never got tired of watching the people go by. Walking around the city made the gears in your brain start turning. People had begun to realize that these simple pleasures were the most delicious part of the fruit we call everyday life, which is why even though their houses were small and food was scarce, they still wanted to live in Tokyo.

Yoshiro felt sure something was wrong: either Amana's head was so full of fruit she could think of nothing else, or her mail was being censored, or she was hiding something from him. Her postcards were frustrating, as if the most important part was covered by the back of an invisible hand, making it impossible to read.

If telephones hadn't disappeared long ago he might have called, though there were actually times when he was grateful for the absence of phones. All their past telephone conversations were arguments that ended with one of them slamming down the receiver. "I hate things that taste sour," Amana would say, and Yoshiro would retort, "You're so fussy about food—that's why you were always catching colds when you were a kid." This would set the girl off. "Force kids to eat stuff they hate and you end up with adults so dull and stupid they don't know what they like," she would scream, prompting Yoshiro to yell back, "I don't remember forcing you to eat anything," giving his daughter ammunition for the next round. With a picture postcard he couldn't fire back immediately no matter what she wrote; besides, knowing at least a week had passed since she'd written it was enough to quell his anger.

Whenever he bought postcards, Yoshiro showed them to Mumei. The pressed flowers, so different from ordinary pictures, their original forms squashed down from three dimensions into two, fascinated the boy. When a postcard came from Okinawa, Yoshiro always told him, "This is from your grandma," which seemed to puzzle him. The

word *grandma* wasn't in his vocabulary, and
remember Amana, the message in invisib
postcard was all he had to go on. Yoshiro cc
ever having said *grandpa*, either. Mumei nev
taching the *great* from *great-grandpa*. To him (
what *Mama* had been to previous generation
had virtually no other family. All the necess
from *Great-grandpa*.

Though Great-grandma was also a farawა
ure to Mumei, the night before her last visit l
excited to sleep, just as he always was right b
Yoshiro, too, had tossed and turned all night.

"What's Great-grandma's name?" Mum
"Marika," Yoshiro mumbled in reply. "Marika
some name," Mumei sighed with a smile, s॰
than his years. His next question, "Where did y
gave Yoshiro pause. The word *meet* didn't seeı
how. Where had he first met Marika, anyway
remember. Back then, they met every week at ș
stration or other. His memories of love began iı
tions. As there was one every Sunday, they prc
prising number of married couples. For some y
demonstrations may have replaced the formal r
ents used to set up with a prospective bride or h

Knowing they'd meet at next week's demons
never bothered to exchange phone numbers o
meet ahead of time. Being fast walkers, they al
up together, ahead of the group. Even when the
huge, stretching for miles behind, after walking a
minutes Yoshiro would find Marika at his side. '

The news of Marika's pregr
sense of happiness; when she su
ined with some trepidation the
to her high-pitched voice and c
of saying in that voice that were
Until she said, "If we do get ı
around much, if that's all right
he began to think that marriage
absent might be bearable after
despised himself for having mɑ
mirable thoughts in mind, so ı
tween them, so much time ha
line between right and wrong h
bered seeing an ice cream make
child, watching the little mixer ş
you put milk, eggs, and sugar iı
"and ice cream comes out below
maker, he and Marika were put
levels below, his great-grandsoı
out. With nothing above, nothiı
low, so things had probably wor
time he thought over this proces
had been not the chef but the inş

Even after their daughter was
home. After breakfast she wou।
baby in the baby carriage along v
bag. She headed straight for a cof
that opened at ten o'clock, where
papers to take to her seat. As the
Marika mouthed the word "Coffε

ing on the counter, read her lips without bothering to come over to her table. Other mothers joined her before long, filling the coffee shop with baby carriages. The air was heavy with exasperated sighs, sharp, needling complaints, high-pitched giggles; voices that rattled off desire after unfulfilled desire, sticky, darkly resentful voices that were also somehow sweet and ingratiating. Around noon Marika would bring home the salad greens she had bought at a nearby Fair Trade Food Shop and quickly fix lunch, which she would eat with Yoshiro, who had spent the morning writing in his study. For the next twenty minutes they would sit face-to-face, husband and wife, sharing an intimate silence, until Marika rapidly did the dishes and left again, pushing the baby carriage. It wasn't so much Marika taking her child outside as this vehicle called a baby carriage taking off on its own, moving ever forward, pulling Marika and all her feelings along after it.

Back then, Yoshiro had been writing a novel about a man who never left the house. Not that he was a shut-in. More like a hermit crab, he got panicky without a house to surround him, so was always racking his brains about how to get interesting people to come visit him.

He thought his wife must find it suffocating being in the house with him, morning to night. That was surely why she cooked up reasons to rush out of the house every morning, pushing the baby carriage.

One morning Yoshiro agreed to meet an editor at a coffee shop, but by the time he'd finished making notes on the project they were to discuss he discovered it was way past the appointed time. When he reached the coffee shop and saw the editor sitting way at the back, shoulders drooping, head down, staring at the translucent skin that had formed on the surface of his milk tea, he wanted to apologize right away but couldn't get to the editor's table. For the whole coffee shop had turned into a parking lot for baby carriages. While babies slept soundly in their mobile beds, mothers talked with furrowed brows. Fragments of conversation, phrases like "recyclable resources," or "afraid my son might turn into a bird," or "putting profit before public health" floated through the air into his ears. While the women were lost in conversation their coffee grew cold in their cups, the cakes they forgot to order dried up inside glass cases, cracks forming in the icing on top. He caught sight of *Pessimism for Mothers* on the cover of a book one of the mothers held in one hand while she had the other thrust deep into her baby's carriage, making circling motions. Sticking his neck out like a giraffe, Yoshiro saw that the mother's hand was rubbing the head of her fidgety infant, round and round, making a tangled mess of the child's hair. Was Marika in another coffee shop like this one, reading and talking? Having a hen party, or a bull session, was she shooting the breeze or just shooting—what was she doing, anyway? Yoshiro finished talking to his editor and left the coffee shop in a state of distraction. He then noticed that the street, too, was full of baby carriages. While Yoshiro had been holed up in his study writing, the whole world had changed. All these children being born, flooding the city with baby carriages, filling the coffee shops with mothers. From beneath their cloth canopies, pacifiers protruding from their mouths like the beaks of birds, their tiny bodies making occasional ripples in their cloth swaddling, the new generation glared resentfully at Yoshiro. So this was what a baby is. If he were to meet his daughter Amana outside would she, too, look this strange? When the light turned green, the white lines of the crosswalk disappeared beneath a torrent of baby carriages. There were baby carriages in front of every bookshelf in all the bookstores; in fact, Yoshiro wasn't able to reach across the three baby carriages blocking his way to get the newly published paperback *In Praise of Masturbation*. Still on tiptoe, he looked down into a baby's eyes, unclouded as a mirror, watching him.

Not long after that, he heard the phrase "Baby Carriage Movement" from Marika for the first time. This was a movement to encourage mothers to push their baby carriages around town every day as long as the sun was shining. Mothers who woke up unbearably miserable every morning, feeling helpless, hungry, about to pee all over themselves with no one to help them, whether because of a moist, clammy dream they'd had the night before, or because being cooped up all day with a squalling infant stimulates memories of the mother's own infancy, went out to push their baby carriages until they came to a coffee shop with a "baby carriage mark" in the window, where they would find books and magazines to read and other mothers to talk to.

When Yoshiro asked her, Marika was more than happy to tell him more about this "Baby Carriage Movement." Pushing a baby carriage was the best way to tell how a town treated its pedestrians. Mothers had to stop if there was no sidewalk, or too many steps. Where the noise was nerve-racking, or there was too much carbon dioxide in the air, the baby would start howling. With lots of other baby carriages around a sort of domino effect kicked in until the collective howling was as

loud as a siren, making passersby stop to think just how un-
pleasant or even dangerous this place was for human beings.
New baby carriages were apparently being developed, with
solar batteries that would recharge while they were outside.

Yoshiro had always been wary of righteous social move-
ments. Milky-smelling virtue contained resentment like sul-
furic acid, directed at male writers too busy penning their
gloomy, perverse novels to think of their homes and families,
and if Yoshiro were to let down his guard, the acid would
surely spill over to burn his hands. Marika, however, had
never criticized him for being a novelist, or even expressed
an opinion about a single one of his books.

Perhaps because she had spent her baby carriage days
breathing the fresh air outdoors, his daughter Amana liked
to walk the streets, even when she had no reason to go out.
As soon as her periods started she began staying out after
dark, but when Yoshiro scolded her for it, she had retorted,
"Thirteen-year-old girls have a better chance of dying at
home than anywhere else. Burglars kill them, or they die
when the whole family commits suicide. The idea that it's
dangerous outside is nonsense."

When she was eighteen Amana abandoned Tokyo to enter a top-level university in northern Kyushu, where she ma-
jored in Organic Studies. She was always going on about how
from the Stone Age until the Edo Period, Kyushu had had
an international flavor. "In Tokyo nature has almost faded
away. I want to live in Southern Japan," she said. Yoshiro
couldn't understand why she said "Southern Japan" instead
of "Kyushu." Even after she graduated, Amana hardly ever
came further north than Shimonoseki. When her son Tomo

came for visits during summer vacation, he was always brought by a friend of Amana's who had business in Tokyo.

With their daughter gone, Marika also moved out, giving work as her reason. She started out at an institution for runaways who didn't want to go back to their parents, later building her own institution in the mountains for children with no one to look after them, which she called "Elsewhere Academy," and settled in as Headmistress. It was rumored that Marika was able to take charge of the place because of her achievements in fundraising, which sounded a little creepy to Yoshiro, who had not only never raised funds of any kind, but couldn't imagine whom you would go to, or how you would get them to cough up such enormous sums of money. As she was his wife he presumably could have asked her, but it was already too late by that time: he had realized that the closer you were to someone the more things you couldn't ask them about. Without arguing, without getting divorced, the two quietly shifted into separation mode. Unable to turn back the clock, they let themselves be turned.

For some time after Amana and her husband moved to Okinawa, their now grown-up son Tomo became a real headache to Yoshiro. On numerous occasions Yoshiro tried to lecture him, but his scolding somehow always turned into a comedy routine, with himself as the straight man.

"What's the most important thing in your life?"

"Can't think of anything really."

"Well, give it some thought, then. When do you feel it's better to be alive than dead?"

"When I'm excited, maybe."

"And when do you feel excited?"

"When I'm doing those three special things."

"What three things?"

"Buying. Throwing. Drinking."*

"You left out the direct objects."

"I have no particular object, directly that is."

"I'm not asking what your object is," Yoshiro fumed, "I'm talking about the grammatical term 'direct object.' What they call the accusative case in German or Russian." Realizing how futile this explanation was, he quickly added, "What do you buy? What do you throw? What do you drink?"

Sneering, Tomo answered, "I buy comics, I throw baseballs, and I drink hot chocolate."

"Idiot! The only thing you're good at is talking nonsense. Why don't you train to be a novelist?"

"I could never do that. I can't stand dead lines."

"Not dead lines—deadlines. Why not be a poet, then? Poets don't have to worry about deadlines—you can write poems whenever you feel like it. Besides, I hear poets are going to be making a lot of money."

"Well, you don't say ... I've never been very good at making money, though."

Nothing he said could wipe the stupid grin off Tomo's face—it was like talking to a bowl of jelly. When Yoshiro got too exasperated to continue the conversation, Tomo would shower him with flattery. "You've got talent, Grandpa, and

* "Buying," coupled with "throwing" and "drinking" would normally mean "buying a prostitute"; "throwing" means "throwing dice" (i.e., gambling).

you only write what you want to write," he'd say. "I envy you, really I do. Keep up the good work."

Not knowing whether to blow up at him or burst out laughing, Yoshiro would just stand there, studying his grandson's well-shaped nose and narrow eyes.

Even when he was still in high school, living at home, Tomo often stayed out all night, and then, after quitting school, he rarely came home at all. Yoshiro sometimes wondered if it wasn't genetic, this desire to find a life outside the family. His wife Marika, his daughter Amana, and his grandson Tomo had all taken off.

Tomo once appeared with a woman as beautiful as a crane in tow. They had come to announce that they were getting married. There wouldn't be a wedding—he would just enter her name in the family register. Several months later, Mumei was born. At the time, Tomo was traveling, so Yoshiro was left alone with the mother and her newborn. The birth was two weeks premature, and the mother had lost so much blood that she had to be rushed, unconscious, to the intensive care unit. The infant was placed in a glass box like a transparent coffin with tubes coming out of his body.

Three days after giving birth, Mumei's mother stopped breathing. Having no idea where Tomo might be, Yoshiro thought it best to postpone the funeral as long as possible. While his mother lay in the "Rest in Peace Deep Freeze" like a wax doll, Mumei, looking more new-boiled than newborn, was taken out of his glass case, supported by the strong, warm, hands of a nurse, to spend his first few weeks of life listening to words of encouragement from Yoshiro.

On the fifth day after the mother's death, Yoshiro was

summoned to the Rest in Peace Deep Freeze to talk with two specialists who had been called in from somewhere faraway. One asserted that because of certain unwelcome changes in the corpse, a speedy cremation would be preferable to preserving it any longer, while the other wanted his permission to dissect the body and preserve it in formalin for research purposes. Yoshiro had no idea what sort of "unwelcome changes" they could be talking about. As none of his questions, phrased in layman's terms, made the image any clearer he took a hard line, insisting that unless he saw the body for himself he wouldn't be able to consent either to cremation or preservation, whereupon the specialists reluctantly escorted him to the body. Unable to believe what he was seeing, Yoshiro gasped and hung his head, covering his nose and mouth with one hand. When he cautiously looked up again, he discovered that this time, the sight of his daughter-in-law didn't shock him nearly as much. The body, in fact, was rather beautiful. Later, however, he found it impossible to reproduce exactly what he had seen. For in his memory, the body continued to mature, to change. The center of the face grew sharper, changing into a bird's beak. The shoulders became more muscular, sprouting feathers like a white swan's. In time, the toes sharpened into chicken's feet.

On the seventh day after her death, the body was carried to the crematorium where a private funeral was held, with only Yoshiro as next of kin. Tomo was still lost somewhere in the mist, while Amana had sent a message saying that since she couldn't make it back in time from Okinawa, Yoshiro should take care of everything. By the time Marika managed to get to the hospital, Mumei was already eleven days old. Yoshiro greeted her standing beside Mumei's bed, chest puffed out, as proud as if he himself had given birth. "A bright looking little fellow, wouldn't you say?" he said, "And handsome, too," but after just a glance Marika took out her handkerchief to wipe away the tears as she ran out of the nursery. Just as Yoshiro started to go after her Mumei started crying, so he stayed with the baby.

After a few days of treating Yoshiro like a visiting relative, the nurses began handing the baby bottle over to him and taught him how to change diapers. He would put the dirty ones into the hamper, and a bunch of clean ones, freshly washed, would be delivered the next day.

"I always thought diapers were made of paper—that you used them once and threw them away," Yoshiro said one day. The nurse in charge of Mumei snorted with laughter that meant "Old people don't know anything," while another coughed and said, "If we used paper for diapers, there wouldn't be enough for novelists to write on." Embarrassed, Yoshiro pulled his head in like a turtle. In no time everyone in the hospital had found out that this old man clumsily changing his great-grandson's diapers actually hid behind a pen name, writing novels.

Though Yoshiro had assumed that only babies without mothers were given formula, he now saw that all the mothers were bottle-feeding their babies. No breast milk was guaranteed to be safe, one of the nurses explained. Breast milk contained, along with its life-giving nutrients, a high concentration of poison. There was no cow's milk in the formula, either.

"What's in it then," Yoshiro asked as a joke. "Wolf's milk?"

"No, but there's bat's milk in it," the nurse replied without cracking a smile. Surrounded by kind nurses who answered all his questions, Yoshiro enjoyed taking care of Mumei at the maternity hospital, yet still wondered why the doctor never appeared until finally he asked the nurse in charge, who seemed to find this question slightly insulting. After giving him her usual "Old people are so out of it" look, she just smiled and said nothing. When he gingerly asked another nurse, she informed him that the distinction between doctors, nurses, and midwives had long since been abolished.

When he raced into the nursery on the thirteenth day after Mumei's birth, Tomo was nearly out of breath. Between gasps he squeezed out a "Grandpa" before lapsing into silence, standing there with tears in his eyes. Hoping he would respond, Yoshiro announced, "This is your son. I've named him Mumei, a name that means 'no name.' Any problems with that?" When Tomo broke down, sobbing like a child, Mumei, who had been fast asleep, burst into tears. The two wailed in perfect unison like siblings who, having both been blamed for starting a fight, start bawling at exactly the same time.

Institutionalized for a serious addiction, Tomo had had no information from the outside until news of his wife's death came, when he had finally been released. Yoshiro refrained from asking whether he had been locked up after getting in trouble with the law or gone voluntarily, or how he was paying for his treatment. "I'll take care of Mumei," he said, as if comforting a child, "so you just take it easy and come back for him when you're well."

With children like this having children of their own, it was no wonder the world was full of children.

Only when Yoshiro said, "I know a place near here so let me treat you to a good meal," did Tomo's face show the hint of a smile. "Thanks, Grandpa," he replied, letting out a wisp of a sigh, then spouting out the lines, "Time sure flies. To think I'm a father now," like an actor in a bad play. You've got a lot of nerve calling yourself that, Yoshiro wanted to scream, but opted to ask, "What exactly are you addicted to, anyway?" instead. "You finally got over watching the doggies run round and round," he went on, referring to his grandson's gambling habits in a deliberately mocking tone, "so is it the little cards with the pretty pictures on them?"

"An addiction as bad as mine isn't limited to any one object. It's metalevel … as long as I can get that feeling of ecstasy, anything will do."

"What did you bet on? Roulette?"

"No, not that."

Blushing, Tomo looked down. This was something he absolutely had to find out, so Yoshiro kept at him until he got an answer, which left him so dumbfounded he gasped for breath before bursting into guffaws of laughter which blew all his anger away.

People say that grandparents love their grandchildren unconditionally, but to Yoshiro, Tomo was a tree that bore only the fruits of anxiety, leaving little time for love, unconditional or otherwise. As a toddler he was always crawling up onto the console of the Total Housework Computer System that almost all homes were equipped with back then to push every button and twist every dial he could reach, plunging the whole house into chaos. Bunch after bunch of frozen spinach would come tumbling out of the freezer to be defrosted, turning the kitchen floor into a green prairie, or the water in the bathtub would get hotter and hotter until the whole bath was at a rolling boil, melting Tomo's rubber ducky into scrambled eggs.

Any machine that made big things happen with just the push of a button or two he loved, while he showed no interest in building blocks, Legos, or swings, either, which he generally gave up on after two or three bends of the knees. Balls did not attract him: he neither caught nor chased them as they rolled along the ground. He didn't listen when picture books were read to him, and the sight of kids his age never made him want to talk or play with them. Pulling their hair to make them cry was all the interaction he could manage. Yet at the sight of a switch he immediately went to flip it, his eyes growing brighter. Which is why Yoshiro wondered if he might be a computer programmer someday—not a bad idea, except that Tomo hadn't the slightest interest in either mathematics or computer technology, caring only for pushing every button he could reach, and then sitting back to watch the grown-ups scurry around, cleaning up the mess. Thinking this anarchistic tendency might be channeled into art, imagining him planning happenings in the future, Yoshiro tried taking him to contemporary art exhibitions and performances. But there seemed to be nothing Tomo hated more than art; in fact, the one time he'd showed a glimmer of interest in a naked dancer, his body painted red all over, performing in an enclosure marked off by brightly colored streamers in the lobby of an art museum, had ended after a few seconds with him scowling, whispering to his grandfather, "More art? Yuck!"

Tomo spent his boyhood wielding virtual swords in battles with big, hairy lizards in digital games, reading Gothic manga sent daily to his cell phone, falling asleep in the beds of soap opera protagonists with the TV still on, and throwing antique vases out the window to smash on the pavement below for no particular reason. At school, his grades hung onto the very end of the balance beam, never quite falling off, but as his classes seemed unbearably long, he was always yawning, opening his mouth so wide his jaw almost came unhinged, or poking the kid in front of him with his pencil, or picking his nose, or looking up at the clock every few seconds, which drove his teachers crazy. "I'd really study in a class that was over in five minutes," he always said. Yoshiro ignored him, assuming he was just trying to get on the nerves of all the grown-ups, but maybe Tomo had been perfectly serious.

Yoshiro sometimes wished that instead of his grandson Tomo were a character in one of his novels. That way there would be no need to get angry, and also much more fun for both writer and readers. Strangely aware of the fact that his grandfather was a novelist though he never read himself, Tomo would brag about that to his friends, showing off copies of Yoshiro's books in his room that he'd shoplifted from bookstores. Though Yoshiro had heard about the schemes where people bet on the next Nobel Prize winner as if they were betting on the races, and knew that enormous sums of money were involved, it never occurred to him that his own grandson would fall victim to this sort of commercial gambling.

"You never even read—what made you think you'd be able to predict the next Nobel Prize winner?"

"When it comes to gambling, a real pro can win in any field!"

"But you just bet on the name some tipster put at the top of a list. Didn't you stop to think maybe the whole thing was set up to get as much money out of as many suckers as possible?"

Because their reunion at Mumei's bedside ended in smiles, it stayed with Yoshiro as a bright, cheerful memory. Tomo returned to the institution, promising to come back clean. The word *clean* had sounded fishy somehow—after all, this wasn't a commercial for laundry detergent, thought Yoshiro, though he hadn't said so aloud.

When Mumei was a month old, Yoshiro carried him home, humming all the while, only to find bad news waiting for him: Tomo had run away from the institution, his whereabouts now unknown. The hope that he had slipped away wanting to see his son's face again slowly revolved like a lighthouse, illuminating the night in all four directions, leaving the sea in darkness.

Yoshiro couldn't decide whether to notify the police or not. He had a favorable impression of the now privatized police force, but positive feelings do not equal trust. The police force's activities now centered on their brass band; they would march in uniform through the streets, swinging their hips from side to side as they performed circus and *chindon-ya* melodies. The band was extremely popular with children, and even Yoshiro was sometimes tempted to follow along behind them. But aside from brass band performances, no one seemed to know exactly what the private police force did. Police boxes on street corners, now renamed "Guide to

Terra Incognito," had nothing to do with the police force. The people stationed in them gave directions, and also provided tourists with information for a fee. Words like *suspect, investigation,* and *arrest* had disappeared from the newspapers. One theory had it that murder was all but unknown since life insurance had been abolished, though Yoshiro had his doubts about this.

He felt sorry for Mumei, with a mother now dead and a father in hiding somewhere, but death and disappearance seemed like private matters and he hesitated to involve the police. Squeezing the baby's tiny hand, shaking it slightly, his desire to laugh and cry at the same time exploded, and out came the words, "We'll hang in there together, chum." Why *chum,* a word he had never used, not even once, until this moment? Perhaps he had wanted to say *comrade,* but after shaking off all the troublesome memories that stuck to it, he was left with *chum* instead.

It turned out to be a good thing he hadn't informed the police. In not very long a letter came from Tomo. "I've left that place behind. Sorry to make you worry. But I have my reasons. The new Head is also the Supreme Leader of the Humananity Cult. More than I can take, really. Dogma filled days. No food made with beans, colored bread is prohibited, part your hair right in the middle. All these sickening rules—really scary. And a whiff of blood in the air. So I ran away. I roughed it for a while, until I ran into someone from my old gang, who brought me to this toy factory. They only hire burnouts like us. The whole factory is set up to look like a casino. Lose and you're a slave; win, you're the boss. The pay's terrible but everything's provided—food, a place to sleep, clothes. Don't know how long it's been since I've had nothing to worry about. The roulette wheels are old but nobody cheats, so I win most of the time."

That was when Yoshiro decided that when Mumei started talking, if he were to ask, "Where's my father?" he would answer, "He lives far away because he's very sick and needs treatment." If he asked what was wrong with his father, he would say, "It's a sickness where you get so stuck on playing one game that you can't do anything else." But so far, Mumei had never shown any curiosity about his parents. When he started school, as none of the other children in his class were being raised by their parents, mothers and fathers were never mentioned.

Children without parents had long since ceased to be called "orphans"; they were now referred to as *doku ritsu jido,* "independent children." Because the Chinese character for *doku* looks like a dog separated from the pack who survives by attaching itself to a human being and never leaving his side, Yoshiro had never felt comfortable with the phrase.

Marika was now head of an institution that housed about fifty "independent children." Though it had a reputation for being well run in spite of severe economic restraints, its dependency on Marika was far from healthy. If she'd ever taken three days off, the whole place would have collapsed like a house of cards. All sorts of vital information was recorded in her brain alone: If, for instance, the farm which usually sent them their vegetables couldn't make a delivery, were there were others that could be relied on, and if not, how could they adjust the menu? Doctors were in short supply, so when a child broke a bone, or had trouble breathing, or diarrhea that wouldn't stop, and no hospital was willing to send a doctor, they needed to find one who'd come, which took an endless supply of knowledge and connections, plus a persuasive tongue—all things that couldn't simply be turned into data and stored away. The extraordinary ability of the human brain to start sifting through a billion stored experiences the moment it senses trouble, picking out all that it needs, then combining and rearranging to reach a conclusion: only this managed to keep the institution afloat.

Marika now wanted to visit Yoshiro and Mumei, to spend an evening talking with them, maybe around a simmering hot pot. Determined to see them, she set about cobbling together a schedule from the few poorly connected trains and buses. She was used to getting up while it was still dark. Every morning, summer or winter, before the sun hooked its fingernails on the horizon and began hoisting itself up, Marika was up, had placed a candle two inches in diameter and four inches tall on the table, and lit it with a match. The orange flame expanded and wavered as if made of rubber, then contracted, writhing. The flame reined in Marika's thoughts, liable to dash off toward the many leftover tasks she had to get out of the way as soon as possible.

That morning, however, she took her bag and left the institution before even lighting a match. The grounds seemed larger than usual as she raced across, chased by vague feelings of guilt at neglecting such an important ritual. Between one streetlight and the next her feet disappeared, absorbed in the darkness. Outside the grounds, where there were no streetlights, she could feel dawn approaching. She hadn't waited for a bus in a long time. As she stared at faraway hills that looked as if they were outlined in India ink, and the shadows of trees, two holes of light opened up in the darkness. The earliest bus had no passengers; and even the driver, who didn't look up when Marika paid her fare, disappeared behind the partition when she sat down. She got off at the train station, the final stop, but in the station saw neither signs nor people. She sat on a cold bench in the waiting room, listening. She was starting to wonder if this was really a station. Based on experience she'd assumed as much, but you couldn't count on things being the way they'd always been. Perhaps this was no longer a station, and she simply hadn't heard the news.

After a while, a man in a top hat and a woman with a large suitcase came through different entrances and, as if they'd arranged it beforehand, sat down on the same bench. Remembering a scene like this from a spy movie she'd seen as a child, Marika watched the pair, trying to figure out if they were really strangers, or somehow connected. In time the waiting room bell clanged loudly, followed by the chuff, chuff of the local nearing the station. As Marika stepped out onto the platform, light raced eastward across the sky like a hunted animal.

Despite knowing how many times she'd have to change trains on this tiring journey, she'd started out feeling sure she'd glide smoothly over the miles to Yoshiro and Mumei. Yet as she sat in room after empty room, waiting for other travelers to make it seem more like a waiting room, then climbed with them into train after train, she lost sight of the end of her trip, almost forgetting why she had set out in the first place. None of the trains sensed where she really wanted to go; they all coldly pushed her out somewhere in the mid-

dle of nowhere. Not that she minded changing trains, it was
the layovers that were so irritating; somehow hers seemed
longer than anyone else's. Had the timetable been arranged
expressly to her disadvantage—if so, by whom, and why?
Marika had a special knack for interpreting the world as a
series of interlocking conspiracies.

At last her train arrived at the final station, where she
waited again for a bus, which jostled her until she got off,
her heart about to burst with a longing that made her lean
forward in spite of herself, her breath coming in puffs as
she made her way between two long rows of prefab houses,
forward, always forward, her steps quickening into a run.
How many identical houses were there in this one block?
The sheer number, and their sameness, was about to wipe
the one house she was looking for out of her mind when
suddenly it came into view. Yoshiro and Mumei were standing out front, waving like beckoning cats, their paws moving
up and down. She used to think that hands should be waved
from side to side like a metronome, but that may have been
due to a steady diet of foreign movies long ago. Two beckoning cats: one big, one tiny. Thanks for beckoning. Suddenly
everything seemed funny to Marika as she leaned forward
even further, laughing as she ran toward them at top speed.

"Great-grandma is here!" Did the joking, whooping voice
that said this belong to Marika herself, her husband, or her
great-grandson? The trio's happiness exploded into joyous
fireworks as they jumped around like rabbits in springtime.
Inside the house, steam was already rising from the clay pot,
waiting for them. Finding the spot in the center of the cushion awaiting her bottom, Marika planted herself in it as if

she were putting down roots. Beyond the cloud of steam, Yoshiro and Mumei looked like wizards in the mist. "Ha ha ha, ha ha ha," laughed Mumei as he stuck his chopsticks into the broth time after time, never managing to catch anything. Fortunately, neighboring chopsticks were always ready to take up the slack, filling his bowl with delicacies from the mountains and the sea. When they found things in the pot they didn't normally eat like shrimp or *maitake* mushrooms, Yoshiro and Marika shook off the dark specter of contamination: casting their nets for sweeter memories, seeking them out even as they crumbled like silken tofu, and not giving up until they'd scooped them into their bowls and devoured them, piping hot. But time showed them no mercy, hurrying on until, with the last forgotten slice of Chinese cabbage lying wilted at the bottom of the pot, the grandfather clock pounded out the hours.

"Ah, I've got to go."

Marika stood up, forced her arms into the scrunched-up sleeves of her jacket, very slowly buttoning it all the way up to the neck though it wasn't very cold, then put on her shoes, which had gotten awfully tight in such a short time, sighing, "Well, I'll see you again sometime, I mean I'd really like to come, you know, if I can, real soon ... but even if it isn't very soon I want to come back no matter what, sometime ..." Her spoken and unspoken words pushed and shoved her until finally, tearing herself away—as if ripping a page from a memo pad, and then crumpling it up to toss into the wastebasket—she started to walk. Her face, drenched with tears, was crumpled too, her voice dying away even as she spoke.

"We'll come see you off," shouted Yoshiro from behind.

He was about to put Mumei on the back of his bicycle when Marika, shielding her face with both hands, said, "You don't need to see me off, I want to leave alone," in a singsong voice meant to hide the tears in her voice. On their own her legs moved faster and faster until they broke into a run, while her elbows—though this wasn't Sports Day for heaven's sake—started pumping up and down as she clenched her teeth, thrust out her chin and ran off, faster and faster. Maybe this is how you'd escape from a fire. Burning meant pain. She'd always hated good-byes and as she grew older she hated them even more. If ripping a bandage off was going to hurt as much as touching the raw wound then maybe you should just leave it on even after it got so dirty it was black and sticky, starting to rot along with your skin, she thought, somewhat childishly.

Neither the rocking of the trains nor the jostling of the buses wiped the image of her great-grandchild's face off of her retinas. Back at the institute, with the pile of undone tasks threatening to spill over in an avalanche, between breaths she still heard Mumei's laughter. The love she should be feeling for all the children here, equally, might thin out, replaced by her obsession with Mumei—that idea terrified her.

Marika had recently been given an important post on the screening committee of a top secret private-sector project she'd been involved with for some time now, selecting especially bright children to send abroad as emissaries. Even among the many in her institute, it would be hard to find one suitable. Smart children who used their intelligence only for themselves wouldn't do. Neither would those who might have a strong sense of responsibility but no aptitude for languages. Speaking well was important, but kids who got drunk on the sound of their own voices were out of the question. Children who could truly empathize with others were disqualified as they'd always be crying in sympathy. Strong-willed children were welcome, but not if they were always forming cliques of underlings to boss around. Kids who couldn't stand being with other people were disqualified, as were those who couldn't bear to be alone. And those lacking the talent and courage to overturn established values as well as rebels, opportunists, the emotionally unstable— none of these would do. No child seemed likely to pass the screening test, except for one perfect candidate.

And she didn't want to send Mumei on a dangerous mission. She wanted to leave him under Yoshiro's protection, living calmly through his days, fighting to the end. No one could say how long he had to live, and there was no need to expose him to undue hardship. If only she kept quiet, Mumei would never be discovered by the screening committee.

Watching the little kids at the institute fall down and burst into tears brought back memories of when her daughter Amana was a little girl, crying all the time. Back then it was widely believed that parents should respond immediately to a child's cries for help: trying to toughen kids up by letting them wail would make them grow up too stubborn to ask for help of any kind, which meant they might not live very long, so as soon as her daughter started to cry, Marika would hold her close, comforting her. But sometimes, when she felt their two bodies connecting by invisible arteries, she'd suddenly pull away.

There was something else she remembered. When Amana was about three years old, she'd taken her back to her parents' house. One day, while they were sitting face-to-face playing cat's cradle in the room with the grandfather clock, she saw capillaries growing out of their bodies like tiny branches. Slender as gossamer from a spider's web, they spread out along the walls and up to the ceiling, twining themselves around the grandfather clock. Quaking in fear, Marika stood up. Until then, she had never seriously thought about the history of that house. Generations of people whose names she didn't know, whom she'd never cared about, had been born and died there. The sweat of women forced to work like slaves drenched the walls; the pillars were splattered with the semen of masters of this house who had forced themselves on young servants. She smelled the cold sweat of a son who had strangled his bedridden father to get his inheritance. The walls and ceiling that had witnessed these atrocities glared down on her. The misery of married couples trickling down into the pipes connecting the toilet to the sewer. A mother who has chemically transformed her loneliness into ambition chokes her son, squeezing his slender neck between her sweaty thighs. A wife who never lets on what she knows about her husband's affairs mixes her own turds into his miso soup. That handsome arsonist seen loitering around the house might be a former employee, fired for no good reason. The umbilical cord binding the generations of a respectable old family is also a rope around the neck. And she had wanted to cut her ties to all these bloody forebearers, now taking such pleasure in sharing old family secrets …

My real family, she thought, are those people I just happened to meet in that coffee shop. My descendants are the independent children in my institution.

The first time Marika saw the simple prefab house where Yoshiro and Mumei had taken refuge, she found it refreshing. Afraid of appearing tactless because, after all, they weren't living there by choice, she hadn't said how attractive she found the house until she started talking to Yoshiro and realized that he, too, was quite pleased with it. It was so simple, with none of the oppressiveness of a sprawling, old family home, or the arrogance of a modern high-rise apartment complex.

They'd been lucky to have good carpenters, Yoshiro told her, who had put up these well-made houses in no time. Other houses just a mile or two away—built by trolls—had poor ventilation, were hotter in summer and colder in winter than it was outdoors, and had walls so thin you couldn't even sigh without the neighbors hearing you, despite having cost three times as much.

The number of temporary houses had increased notably in the area from Tama to Nagano Prefecture; it was predicted that more and more people would be moving into the land along the Nakasendo, the old road through the mountains that leads to Kyoto. Central Tokyo was deserted. Although no one had heard anything about an evacuation of the Diet or the Supreme Court, the buildings that had housed them were definitely not in use. They were empty shells. When the Japanese government was privatized it was rumored that all the Diet members and judges had taken their generous pensions and moved to a newly constructed high-class residential area in Kyushu called "Satsuma Forest." But where did the newly elected Diet members work? Did they really exist, or were they simply photographs with names? Yoshiro remembered going to City Hall, which doubled as Election Hall, writing a name on a piece of paper, and duly submitting his vote. That much, at least, had really happened. The pencil he'd used to write the name had definitely been real.

The Diet's main job was to fiddle around with the laws. Judging from how often the laws changed, someone was definitely fiddling with them. Yet the public was never told who made the changes, or for what purpose. Afraid of getting burned by laws they hadn't heard of, everyone kept their intuition honed sharp as a knife, practicing restraint and self-censorship on a daily basis.

When the public was informed that the isolation policy had already gone into effect, Yoshiro and Marika weren't the only ones too shocked to do anything but gasp and moan. Yet every newspaper ran articles declaring, "There were many good things about the Edo period. Isolation is not necessarily a bad policy." And many of the public intellectuals who wrote these articles—though actually opposed to isolation—found the humiliation of having the policy so suddenly sprung on them unbearable, as if they were being made to eat dirt; besides, if they admitted they'd been duped like everybody else their careers would be ruined, so now, in an about-face so obvious it would have amazed even Aesop's grape-loving fox, they all insisted that they had supported isolation all along and in fact had been just about to recommend it to the government.

When Yoshiro submitted an essay entitled "Japan Was Not Isolated" to the newspaper, they refused to publish it. He wrote it to show how strong Japan's connections to the outside world had been during the Edo period, through the channels of Holland and China, but the newspaper's official scholar refused to give it his stamp of approval. He decided to hang onto the manuscript until the next time a magazine asked him for a contribution, yet strangely enough, all those requests from magazines dried up completely after that.

In a fit of anger, Yoshiro dashed off a children's story, which he promptly sent to a publisher he'd worked with. It was about a little girl in the sixth grade. In the country where she lived, it was decreed that all children must bring a lunch of white rice with a red pickled plum in the middle to school. So every morning, the girl's mother pressed a pickled plum into the middle of the white rice in bento boxes for the girl and her little brother, with a dark sheet of dry *nori* seaweed hidden under the surface. In a separate container, she packed things to go with the rice, like cold omelettes or spinach. One day, the girl's mother was injured in a car accident and had to spend the night in the hospital. Her father, away on a business trip, couldn't make it home right away. The little brother cried himself to sleep that night, so the next morning, to cheer him up, the girl cut the paperlike *nori* into the shapes of a panda's eyes and ears to put on his rice. Extremely pleased with his panda lunch, the boy proudly showed it to his classmates. The following morning, his older sister was sent to a youth detention center, and her mother, now out of the hospital, was arrested.

Unfortunately, Yoshiro's children's story has yet to be

published. The letter from the publisher said, "The content is incomprehensible to children."

Under the cool silk bedding pulled up to her nose, Marika sometimes giggled, remembering when she and Yoshiro used to have sex. That had been more than eighty years ago. The images that came to her were more like dinosaurs at play than of erotic ecstasy between the sheets.

Marika's skin and general bearing were still youthful, though inside, her body had changed completely. Long ago she had felt as if her nipples were being pulled outward, while now her breasts were spreading out, expanding inward, protecting the front from enemy attack. When she was young, perhaps because her nerve endings hadn't reached that far back yet, her bottom was always the coldest part of her—in fact, when someone gave her butt a pat she was surprised at how far her own body bulged out in the rear—yet now her whole backside was always hot and haughty, issuing orders: "Get off me and open a window, NOW!" or "You'd better set yourself down on me and check those receipts again." They used to say that henpecked husbands were "under the wife's bottom," and now Marika felt definitely under her own.

"The whole human race is becoming feminized," asserted some specialists, while others said, "Children who are born male turn into females, while those born female turn into males."

In areas where culture dictated that female fetuses should be aborted, Nature, enraged at humans disrupting her balance this way, had started playing various tricks. One trick was making sure that no one stayed the same sex all their lives. Everyone's sex changed either once or twice, and people couldn't tell ahead of time how many times their sex would change.

Yoshiro set the New Year's photo Marika had sent on top of the chest of drawers. A child with half-closed eyes rested a heavy looking head on his wife's left shoulder. From the expression, the child might have been either in pain or simply daydreaming. Long, thick eyelashes, lips like cherries, a very slender neck with an oddly well-developed Adam's apple protruding from it. In comparison, Mumei's neck looked positively sturdy, set firmly on his shoulders. The child with both hands on Marika's other shoulder had its chin thrust out, sticking its tongue out at the camera. Another was asleep with its head on her knees, while still another knelt properly on the tatami, acting the model student. The sharp-eyed kid in the background might have been feverish, its face was so red. Several others didn't even seem aware that they were being photographed. Though they all looked like girls, some were probably boys.

When Marika's longing to see Yoshiro and Mumei rose like the tide, she forced it into the small rectangular space of a picture postcard, waiting for it to ebb. On a recent card she'd written, "How are you two getting along? I'll bring a big sea bream made of sugar for your 108th birthday."

Yoshiro didn't really feel like making concrete plans for his 108th birthday party. But he did want to hear Mumei shout, "Paradise!" It would be fun to get into their bathing suits for a fountain party, or dress up like ghosts and set off sparklers in the evening. His ninety-ninth birthday, when all his relatives had gathered, seemed like a long time ago now. It was good that he'd picked ninety-nine rather than one hundred, but the standard birthday dinner around a big, round table at a restaurant had been a mistake. You could tell the younger relations by their rounded backs, thinning hair, pale faces, and by how slowly their chopsticks moved. Realizing their descendants were in such a sad state because they'd been so feckless made the elderly feel guilty, dampening the festivities.

While it wasn't clear whether or not Yoshiro's generation would really have to live forever, for the time being they had definitely been robbed of death. Perhaps when their bodies had reached the end, even their fingers and toes worn down to nothing, their minds would hang on, refusing to shut down, writhing still inside immobile flesh.

Yoshiro couldn't see why his generation should celebrate long life. It was good to be alive, but that was normal for the elderly, so why make a fuss about it? With children dying off this way, wouldn't it make more sense to celebrate a child's having got through another day? He wanted to celebrate Mumei's birthday not once a year, but every season. A party for each winter he managed to make it through without getting frostbite. Or for every autumn after he'd gone a whole summer without collapsing from the heat. At the turn of the season the body sloughs off old stuff and takes on new life. Yoshiro felt younger when spring came, but the change was always hard on Mumei. It took extra energy to meet a new season. And that wasn't the only kind of change that was challenging for Mumei. He'd be bathed in sweat from temples to armpits in suffocating heat on a summer day with the temperature rising, so high it seemed it would never fall, but then the air would dry out a little and he'd be shivering as if he'd been stripped to the skin. The sun had only to peek through the clouds for his skin to dry up and crack; a drenching in an evening shower left him shivering right down to the bones. Every bit of food he put in his mouth was a challenge to be met. If sour orange juice bit into his stomach wall, he'd lose all its nourishment and burden his digestive system as well. Taking a breather after yesterday's grated carrot, his stomach would then be desperately battling today's bean fiber, not producing enough digestive juices to win, which caused Mumei's tummy to swell up with gas.

Always worried, always watching, Yoshiro took his own chin in his left hand and forced himself to look off in another direction. If he kept his eyes glued on him, the boy's spirit might possess his great-grandfather and then turn him into a poor eater. Then who would look after Mumei? He kept trying to convince himself that his generation were an entirely different species from kids today, tough enough both physically and mentally to work from morning to night without ever getting sick or even tired.

Though he was always on the lookout for food Mumei could eat without too much trouble, he never bought new products unless he knew where they came from. Once thousands of dead penguins had washed up on a beach in South Africa, and a company run by an international pirate gang had dried the meat, which it then ground into powder to make meat biscuits for children. According to the newspaper, another company was smuggling the biscuits into Japan, making a killing. The biscuits reminded Yoshiro of dog food, but having heard they were an ideal protein source for children, he definitely wanted to buy some. The meat of penguins who had lived in Antarctica would probably not be very contaminated, though such a mass death might mean that an oil tanker had sunk nearby, which was worrying.

Having left the country without permission, Japanese pirates in the international gangs did not have the right to return. "I'd rather be a pirate with guys from all over the world than go back to Japan. I make more money and besides, it's safer," wrote one Japanese pirate in a letter to the newspaper. Yoshiro laughed out loud when he read it. If a letter like this could still appear in the newspaper, then freedom of speech was not yet extinct, unlike the Japanese crested ibis.

While it didn't seem all that strange for Norwegians or Swedes, with their Viking heritage, to join pirate gangs, people from countries like Nepal, or Switzerland, with no connection to the sea, were also joining up. And the sizable number of Japanese pirates suggested that there was no gene for isolation.

The South African government announced it would take a firm stance against all forms of piracy. Yoshiro had heard about international pirate gangs at a lecture entitled "The Future of Sharks and the Prospects for Fish Cakes." Because lectures weren't censored, they were a source of raw information unavailable anywhere else. Yoshiro went to every lecture within walking distance, about six miles from home. Public lectures were always packed.

South Africa and India—having been among the first countries to withdraw from the global rat race in which huge corporations turned underground resources into anything they could sell at inhuman speeds while ruthlessly competing to keep the lowest production costs—now kept to a policy of supporting their economies by exporting language alone, discontinuing all other imports and exports. The two nations had formed what they called "The Gandhi Alliance," which was gaining worldwide popularity. They got along so well that other countries were beginning to envy them. South Africa and India fought about soccer but nothing else, their positions on humanity, the sun, and language being perfectly matched. Contrary to the predictions of foreign experts, the economies of both were growing steadily.

Like these two nations, the Japanese government had also stopped importing underground resources and exporting manufactured goods, but with no language to export, it had come to an impasse. So the government had hired a linguist to write a paper proving that the language Okinawans spoke was linguistically unrelated to Japanese, to promote its plan to sell the Okinawan language to China for a good price, but Okinawa refused to let this underhanded scheme go through. They came back with an ultimatum: If Japan insisted on selling their language to China, then Okinawa would stop all shipments of fruit to the main island of Japan.

While Yoshiro's mornings were packed full of worry seeds, to Mumei each morning was fresh, full of fun. At the moment, he was battling those mischievous sprites called clothes. Though cloth was not necessarily ill-tempered, it didn't bend easily to his will, and as he tried rubbing it, smoothing it over, folding it, but generally having a hard time, bits of brightly colored paper—orange, blue, and silver—began to sparkle in the gray matter of his brain. He wanted to take off his pajamas, but with two legs he couldn't decide which to start with, and while he was puzzling over this problem he remembered the octopus. Maybe he had eight legs, too, and it just looked like two because each one was a bundle of four, tied tightly together. That might be why when he tried to move one leg to the right he felt like swinging it at the same time to the left, or sticking it up in the air. There was an octopus inside him: *Octopus, get out of there!* He pulled off his pajama pants. He couldn't have pulled his legs off with them, could he? No, they were still attached—it was only his pajamas that had come off. So far, so good, but he still had to get into his trousers for school. They were a mountain of cloth, with tunnels running through it. His legs were the trains, trying to get through the tunnels. He sure wanted to go back to the Meiji Restoration Museum and play with the model steam engine again. There were two tunnels, so the train headed for Tokyo can go in one, while the train going in the opposite direction comes out the other. That must be it, but although his right leg went in okay, his left leg didn't come out. Oh, well, who cares? Flesh-colored steam engines slide into the tunnels. Chugga chugga choo choo.

"Mumei, are you dressed yet?"

At the sound of Great-grandpa's voice, the octopus scuttled off to hide in his socks as the trains slid off the rails, leaving Mumei there all alone. He hadn't yet completed the task of getting dressed.

"I guess I'm not much of a man," he sighed gravely, prompting Yoshiro to burst out laughing as he urged, "Don't worry about that now, just hurry up and put your pants on—here," bending over to take the trousers in both hands and spread them out.

"I wish I could have some work clothes like we saw that time."

"Work clothes? Oh, you mean a *tsunagi*. People used to call tsunagi overalls."

"Overalls … sounds awesome."

"But *overalls* is a foreign word, so you'd better not use it."

"Better not use it" was a phrase that never sounded right to Mumei. Great-grandpa knows lots of words; he never uses lots of the words he knows; he teaches me words he never uses; then he tells me never to use certain words he tells me about. Great-grandpa blurred into several overlapping faces. Could clothes still be there, just as they were, even after the words for them had disappeared? Or did they change, or disappear, along with their names? "I don't want pants with elastic in them," Mumei had protested the week before at a children's clothing store, "They leave diamonds around my waist that get itchy." He had begged for overalls, but was refused on the grounds that a tsunagi would be too much trouble when he went to the bathroom by himself at school. When he'd seen the one on a plumber who came to their house once, he'd been so envious he'd never forgotten it. After refusing to buy him a tsunagi, Great-grandpa had stayed up all night making a special pair of trousers for him.

"If you don't hurry up you'll be late."

That's what Great-grandpa always says. It's not that I hate school, but having to get dressed in a hurry and be there by a certain time sure doesn't make me like it. It takes time to get ready, but that's not my fault. Clothes, juice, shoes—they all do their own thing, and never help me out. It's the same with the clock. The hands keep on moving at their own pace, never thinking of me at all. Why can't we just go to school when we feel like it? The best thing about school is that there're lots of other kids to play with, but the worst thing is that they bother you when you're trying to learn. You can study much better by yourself. Whenever I have something really important to tell the teacher, some other kid always yells something stupid so he can't hear me. The kid behind me pulls my hair while I'm thinking, and whenever the teacher starts to tell us something interesting somebody yells, "I gotta pee!" and that's the end of it. Counting up the things I hate about school, I can't wait for Earth Day, when I can stay home all day. How many times do I have to poop until another day without school comes around? Every morning, Great-grandpa eggs me on. "Come on, push. A good BM means you have the strength to fight against germs." Today's Tuesday. Tuesday is fire day, so maybe we'll do an experiment with matches in science class. I'll probably get burned. Tomorrow's Wednesday, water day. I might drown in the heated pool. I wish they'd turn up the heat. It's so cold now it makes me want to scream at first, but if I make too much of a fuss I get so tired my legs go all wobbly like noodles and I can hardly walk. "If you're tired just lie down beside the pool and rest awhile," the teacher says, but don't grown-ups ever notice that the pool has tides? I'll be lying down as the waves get higher and higher until they come right up over the edge, and splash, splash, splash, right in my face. Then a great big wave will come to swallow me up. I'll gasp and lift my head up, trying to breathe, but the wave pulls my wrists and ankles down to the bottom.

But wait—oh, yeah, I know what to do next: I'll just turn myself back into an octopus. No need to be afraid of the water, I'll get through water day as an octopus, and wait for Thursday—tree day. On tree day maybe the cherry tree in the schoolyard will fall on top of me and crush me. Almost all the trees are sick these days, even if they look healthy their trunks are hollow, so all it takes to make them fall over is a sigh from someone standing near. That's why all those signs say "Do not sigh near this tree." I can see it now—a whole row of cherry trees falling like dominoes, starting with the one farthest away. I run away. I'm so fast not even one branch hits me. Sure feels good, running like that. Friday is gold day. The sun has only one eye, bright yellow like gold, and when it glares down on me my whole body goes so stiff I can't move. That's why I'm not allowed to play outside by myself. I can see the cliff behind our school crumbling … with me caught in the landslide. No one comes to help me. My elbows get numb. There's no feeling in my legs; when I touch them they seem like somebody else's …

"Mumei, want some toast?"

The rye bread Great-grandpa toasts for me smells good, but it's sure hard to chew. The mean little spikes of dried grain stick into the soft places inside my mouth all at once. I taste blood. Grain—even after you pick it, thresh it, grind it up into powder, knead it, and bake it—is still spiky—it never gives up. How stubborn can it be? Once when I said, "This toast tastes like blood," Great-grandpa looked like he was about to cry, so I decided never to say that again. Great-grandpa has real bushy eyebrows and a square jaw, so he looks strong, but his feelings get hurt real easily, and he of-

ten looks like he's about to cry. For some reason he seems
to pity me.

But anyway, how can old people chomp away at hard bread
that way as if there's nothing to it? People used to have really
strong teeth. They used to make what they called "extra-
hard rice crackers," as hard as rocks, just to munch on. Once
Great-grandpa pretended to be chewing on a stone-hard rice
cracker to make me laugh. It would have been even funnier
with the real thing but he told me they don't sell them anymore. He used to open his mouth wide, put the rice cracker
between his teeth, and then pull down on the part outside so
that cracker, round as the moon, would go *gagariiin,* and snap
in two. Then his tongue would move the piece in his mouth
back to his molars so they could break it up into little bits,
just like smashing rocks. They say if the walls in an apartment building were thin enough you could hear the people
next door eating rice crackers. Not just rice crackers. Those
old people who could break roasted almonds or bite off bits
of dried meat with their teeth must have been just like squir-
rels, or lions. I guess you couldn't put me and Great-grandpa
on the same page in the *Illustrated Guide to Animals.*

The old folks used to eat bird's innards and pregnant river
fish, roasted on skewers over open flames, too. I couldn't believe it at first, but watching Great-grandpa I started to realize it might be true. He's put together so completely different
from us kids. Great-grandpa doesn't just eat hard things, he
eats so much I can't believe it. That's why he has energy to
spare. He runs around after he gets up in the morning, to
burn off his extra energy. We kids don't have even a single
drop to spare. If I spend too much energy getting dressed I

don't have enough left to walk to school and end up riding on the back of Great-grandpa's bicycle. It's embarrassing to ride all the way so I always try to walk at least the first ten steps or so, but my legs get so heavy I can't walk anymore.

"Mumei, aren't you dressed yet? You'll be late for school," Great-grandpa says, coming over to me. I know he's trying to sound strict, but I'm not the least bit afraid.

Yoshiro inhaled the fragrant child smell that rose from the back of Mumei's neck. That was it—this smell. When his daughter Amana was a baby, this was what he smelled when he picked her up, cradling her tiny body close. At the time he'd thought it was a little girl smell, but Mumei had it too, even more strongly. After Amana grew up, she had Tomo. Even now Yoshiro remembered the time she asked him to put the child's socks on, how precious those tiny feet had looked as he fitted the socks over them, like covering particularly valuable apples with protective wrappings. Nevertheless, Tomo had never smelled as good as Amana. Even as a toddler, the smell he gave off was already mixed with mud and sweat. By the time he started elementary school he had abandoned socks; sticking his bare feet into gym shoes he'd flattened the backs of, he'd run outside to play whenever he wanted, without even bothering to say, "I'm going out." Never quiet, never polite, but he had certainly been a sturdy lad.

"Don't you love your own child?" Yoshiro had blurted out, soon after Mumei's birth—a corny thing to say, really, but Tomo had startled him by firing back, "How do you know he's mine?" He had immediately consigned this remark to the furnace of oblivion, doubting he'd find the truth in the middle of an argument, but as time passed, he heard a voice, whispering from the ashes. Tomo himself didn't know whether or not he was Mumei's father.

Mumei's mother was neither a penguin nor a lovebird. Ignorant of chastity, she was always willing, never faithful, oblivious of condemnation, with no sense of sin, and she drank like a bottomless serpent. Now reduced to ashes, she couldn't be asked about Mumei's parentage. Even if she were alive, she probably wouldn't remember.

Knowing there was a possibility they were not genetically related, Yoshiro had once considered sending a lock of Mumei's hair to the hospital to be tested, but one day, feeling some hairs he'd picked up from the tatami between his fingers, he started to chuckle. Genes have no odor. Yet how well he knew that sweet, milky fragrance of infancy that still rose from Mumei's body. It was clearly sending him a message. Neither of the child's parents had ever gotten drunk on that smell the way he did. Didn't that mean that Nature herself had chosen him, Yoshiro, as Mumei's guardian?

Yoshiro heard singing from the house next door, a girl's voice about to melt into the blue sky.

"Dragonfly, how do you fly, dragonfly?"

The clear, high *dra* of "dragonfly" reverberated in Yoshiro's head. Had the owner of that sweet young voice ever seen a dragonfly? Probably not. Yoshiro himself couldn't remember the last time he'd seen one. Yet an unseen dragonfly lived in this little girl's song. Its translucent wings and long, pencil-thin, segmented body would zip through the air, then stop, hovering for a second before taking off in a completely unexpected direction. Dragonflies were so mysterious, stopping in midair that way. Just once, Yoshiro wanted to show Mumei a real one.

He heard the little girl's voice clearly through the prefab walls. When she'd finished her song, a woman's voice said, "We'd better be leaving for school now." He'd seen the girl with this woman who looked after her out front on their way to school. But as the child was always dressed in what looked like a white spacesuit, he had never seen her face. Yoshiro assumed the suit was solar energy-propelled musclewear, though when Mumei sighed, "Doesn't she look beautiful?" he had to admit that, yes, there was definitely something about the suit that made the word *beautiful* seem just right. Maybe this was the beauty of the future. Yoshiro remembered how girls used to choose clothes that would emphasize the curve of their waists or the size of their breasts, leaving their thighs or the backs of their necks exposed whenever possible. As he watched this little girl float down the sidewalk like a cloud the word that came to mind was not *sexy* but *elegant*.

Although the girl left for school around the same time as Mumei, she went to an elementary school attached to a research institute, attended only by children who had been chosen. Apparently all gifted in some way, they received specialized education.

Her adult guardian didn't indulge in everyday conversation, always turning away after a perfunctory bow. Long ago Yoshiro would have tried to break the ice by noting how hot or cold it was, or how it looked like rain, but talking about the weather had become very tricky. Heat and cold mingled together into a dry humidity, taunting the skin. As if making fun of the very words human beings used to describe the weather. The minute you said, "It's very warm" you'd be shivering; no sooner were the words "It's awfully nippy this morning" out of your mouth than your forehead would be damp with sweat.

A month before, someone had put up a poster on the wall outside the elementary school: NO ONE SPEAKS OF THE WEATHER ANYMORE OR REVOLUTION EITHER. In bold fancy lettering, it was a take on the famous quotation, WHILE PEOPLE SPEAK ONLY OF THE WEATHER I SPEAK OF REVOLUTION—but the very next day someone took it down.

And it wasn't just hot and cold—the difference between darkness and light was also becoming vague. Thinking what a gloomy day it was, you'd be staring up at a gray sky, which would brighten as if illuminated by a light bulb hidden somewhere deep inside until the sky was so blindingly bright you had to turn away. You'd narrow your eyes on what seemed like a really windy day, then the air would freeze and stop moving altogether. As the sun was setting, the outlines of the roofs would light up. You'd turn the light on inside because it was too dark to read the newspaper, and as the paper absorbed all the light, the newsprint would disappear in darkness. At bedtime you'd turn off the light, only to find the moon so bright you couldn't get to sleep. Wondering how it could possibly be that bright you'd open a window to find the moon wasn't even out. It would only be the lead of a pencil left in the road that looked as if it was shining. Streetlights and lights in the houses would all be out, as if urging the night to *act like night already,* but be all that as it may, why was the dawn breaking in what certainly looked like the dead of night?

While Mumei was putting his shoes on, Yoshiro approached the yard next door from the south side, following the sound of the girl's voice. Temporary houses didn't have fences or hedges. Craning his neck to peer inside, Yoshiro saw a chest of drawers and a desk placed primly on the tatami, but no sign of people. Ten empty cans were lined up on the windowsill, each four inches tall, each with a small flower in it. A purple bell, a yellow pitcher, a red firecracker, a white whim, a scarlet stain. "Mumei would love this series of colors, maybe I should line our windowsill with flowers too," he was thinking when he heard a voice from behind say, "Good morning." Startled, he turned to see the woman who lived there, wearing a red silk dress with her white hair done up neatly in a bun, pushing a wheelchair toward him. The girl, in a white dress today instead of the space suit, sat in the wheelchair, smiling. Her dark eyes sometimes looked azure, depending on the light. Her eyes were very far apart. Perhaps that was what made him feel dizzy, looking at her. He wished Mumei could talk to her.

"Excuse me. I was just having a look at your flowers. Lovely, aren't they? Would you like to meet my great-grandson sometime?" Yoshiro asked, slowly walking backwards as the two nodded, moving toward him. Mumei, squatted down beside Yoshiro's bicycle, was slowly revolving the pedals with his hands.

"Mumei, say hello to our next-door neighbor," Yoshiro said, then turning to the girl asked, "Could you tell me your name?"

"I'm Suiren," she answered, nodding once to Mumei. There was confidence in the gesture, making her seem much older than Mumei although they were the same age. Leaning forward, Mumei walked unsteadily over to the wheelchair.

"This is my great-grandson Mumei. He's glad to meet you," he said. He was regretting not having let the boy introduce himself when Mumei, pointing at his great-grandfather, chirped, "This is Yoshiro. He's glad to meet you."

"My name is Nemoto," the woman introduced herself, carefully pronouncing each syllable while leaving her relationship to Suiren unclear. Mumei couldn't take his eyes off the girl. Not the least bit shy, he stared at her, nor did he seem to mind her staring back. Watching them embarrassed Yoshiro, who finally took Mumei by the hand, saying, "If we don't leave for school soon you'll be late," and led the boy back to their house, where he wiped the bicycle oil off Mumei's hands with a Japanese towel soaked in antiseptic.

Because Mumei's birdlike legs turned inward from the knee down, he turned them outward as he walked, step by step. He kept his balance by making big circles with his arms as his school bag, the strap slung diagonally from one shoulder across his chest, flapped lightly at his slender waist. While Yoshiro pushed the bicycle, Mumei walked at his side.

Yoshiro walked as slowly as he possibly could, trying his best to make it seem as if this was his natural pace. Mumei, in turn, pretended not to notice that Yoshiro was walking slowly on purpose.

When Mumei stopped, Yoshiro stopped too. After a while, Mumei would start again. Then, after about ten steps or so, he would stop. Each step was hard labor.

Day by day Mumei was storing up muscles in some unseen place. Not the sort that bulged so everyone could see them, but muscles he needed to walk in a way known only to himself, muscles that spread, little by little, throughout his body like a net. Yoshiro was starting to think that maybe the way human beings had always walked, upright on two legs, wasn't the best way after all. Just as people had stopped riding in cars, perhaps they would stop walking on two legs one day, and invent a completely different way of moving. When everyone was scuttling across the ground like octopi, Mumei might be an Olympic athlete.

Shaking off his daydream, Yoshiro stopped the bicycle and put down the stand. "You really walked a lot today. Much further than yesterday," he said as he slipped his hands under Mumei's arms to lift him up, wincing as he always did at how light the boy was, then gently placed him on his little throne, firmly attached to the back carrier. It had a soft cushion to sit on, a backrest that reached all the way up to his head, armrests, footrests, and a green seatbelt, as well as other features. Yoshiro pedaled off, putting his weight behind it.

The open space in front of the school was as busy as a morning market. After Yoshiro lifted him down, Mumei walked straight toward the building without looking back.

Guardians were permitted to accompany children to their classrooms, but as usual Yoshiro watched Mumei's back for about three seconds before leaving as if driven away.

Once inside, Mumei took off his shoes and placed them neatly in the shoe rack with the heels touching. No one wore shoes indoors. The children walked down the corridor in cotton socks, feeling the cool of the wood under their feet until they came to a row of classrooms with tatami floors. The wooden boxes piled up in the corner of each room served as desks when necessary. There were no chairs. As soon as Mumei reached his classroom he fell upon the first classmate he saw like a playful puppy. Several other pairs of kids were clasped together in leisurely wrestling matches, most of them girls. None fell in a clumsy way. Keeping their hips low to the ground, they curled up like hedgehogs when someone pushed them over. Nervous guardians who'd been afraid at first that the kids would hurt themselves soon realized that they were pretty much immune to injury.

The blue silk scarf around Yonatani's neck felt hot, almost suffocating until he finally loosened it. Sure he'd lose it if he left it that way, he tied it tight around his left wrist. Now I look like a wounded soldier, he thought. That was when his eyes met Mumei's, sitting on the tatami looking up at him. The boy was staring at the scarf as if it were strange indeed.

"Why did you take off your scarf, Mr. Yonatani?"

"Because I'm hot."

"Hot?"

"That's right. Sometimes I suddenly feel very hot, or very cold. It's a sort of menopausal disorder."

"What's a men-oh-paw-zal-dis-order?"

"It's when your body changes keys. You know, the way music sometimes changes from a major to a minor key."

Though in the old days you hardly ever heard of men suffering from menopause, the number of men whose symptoms were so severe they had to take time off from work had increased in recent years. That very morning, Yonatani had been reading the paper, an article about social problems, when he'd suddenly started shivering, his hands and feet like ice. He'd put on his socks, pulled a heavy jacket over his shoulders, and was drinking hot coffee when the heat in his throat began to spread through his body until sweat was running down his forehead, forcing him to throw off the jacket. To cool down his head, now like a kettle about to boil, he had come to school in his shirtsleeves. As soon as he entered the building he heard the kids screaming as they horsed around together—cries of joy, he knew, but his heart raced just the same. Ten years before he'd never been aware of the beating of his own heart.

Yonatani no longer believed as he had when he'd first started teaching that the children would hurt themselves if he wasn't watching them all the time. Even that kid Mumei, who looked like he was about to fall over any minute, knew to lower his center of gravity before stretching out both hands to drape himself over Yasukawamaru's back. He'd warned Yasukawamaru he was coming, too, with a high-pitched cry that sounded like a crane, giving the other kid time to slowly turn around to see who was coming up behind him. It was more like watching a carefully choreographed dance than two kids fighting.

A few steps away from the kids, Yonatani stood watching them play. Realizing how straight he was standing, his back stiff as a ramrod, he quickly squatted down to survey the classroom from a lower angle. When he was young, tall men had still been favored in Japanese society. This prejudice had obviously been imported from abroad, through foreign movies and magazines. Then, at the end of the Heisei Era, with society changing at the speed of pebbles rolling down a steep hill, memories of the Edo period rose up from dilapidated graveyards to dispel the notion that tall men had the advantage, for back then, in lean years the tallest were always the first to sicken and die.

Yonatani didn't even know who the tallest kid in his class was. The yearly ritual of measuring children's height had been abolished. When he heard other teachers say it was inhuman to stretch children out to measure their length as if they were pieces of cloth or string, Yonatani thought they had a point. Kids should be left to curve and bend as much as they liked. While playing freely like puppies, each child could develop the particular kind of strength he or she needed.

When Yonatani was a boy, there were lots of kids who couldn't move without a scenario called "sports." He himself had joined the neighborhood Little League baseball team at the age of five, the soccer club in junior high school, and in high school, the basketball club. They had practice eight days a week. When he told his class that the kids had burst out laughing, saying, "A week has only seven days!" but back then, following their coach, who was always growling, "As far as you're concerned, a week has *eight* days," they had duly tried to cram two days into one every Sunday, eating and doing their homework at twice the normal speed between morning and afternoon practice sessions. One morning during the first semester of his second year in high school, when the cherry blossoms were in full bloom, he'd found he couldn't get out of bed, or even put on his socks, and that was when he'd quit the basketball club.

All through his childhood and youth, he'd kept his body moving, chasing after balls with his friends, yet he had almost no memory of touch, of his heart beating faster after coming into physical contact with another boy. Not only other kids, even his own body had seemed to be moving on some two-dimensional plane like an anime character he could watch but never really touch. The closest thing to a sensual memory he had was of putting his hand into his catcher's mitt, that slight thrill he felt every time his skin touched leather, bringing the mitted hand up to his nose when the others weren't watching to breathe in the earthy aroma. Once when a classmate called Michiru had left her hand lying on top of her desk, he had touched it by mistake. He'd pulled away immediately, but the shock of feeling her warm, moist flesh stayed, carved into his memory. After that he was always aware of Michiru, so much so that even when the classroom faded into black and white boredom, she alone appeared in living color. Every time Michiru said someone's name he was listening, he examined every letter on all her school papers, watched everything she did at recess. That single touch, apparently, had stolen the key to his heart.

Watching the kids in his class, Yonatani was sure they had evolved far beyond his own generation. Just as playful wrestling matches helped make lion cubs strong enough to survive on the savanna, these children were learning about the earth through physical contact. If he were to give a name to this first morning class, it would be "spontaneous romping." Yonatani considered his main job as homeroom teacher to be careful observation. Not supervision—observation.

Mumei threw himself on top of a group of boys sitting close together, sprawling out to cover them, trying out all the techniques of his special octopus-fighting method. When he was out of breath, he retreated to a corner of the classroom to hang his homemade COME BACK LATER sign around his neck. This was his way of keeping his classmates from bothering him when he needed to rest. He'd gotten the idea from a sign he'd seen on the door of a neighborhood noodle shop. Her head tilted coquettishly, Karo-chan sidled up to him and asked, "What does that mean?" He'd explained it to her just the other day and here she was, back again with the same silly question. A little put out, Mumei replied sharply, "I told you that yesterday," but Karo, apparently not the least bit embarrassed, said, "I forget." How could she possibly forget that fast? Convinced she must be laughing at him, Mumei snapped back a little too loudly, "Quit teasing me!" He heard a wail, loud as a siren. As soon as he realized it was Karo-chan bawling, he felt an invisible hand slap his cheek, and in a flash, understood that not everyone's brain works in the same way.

"I'm sorry," he apologized, "it means we're closed for the time being, so don't come into our shop," repeating his explanation from before, word for word. Though it had satisfied her then, today she needled him: "Sounds weird—you're not a noodle shop, you know." So that was their strategy—

ask the same question, get the same answer, but by reacting a little differently each time, worm your way in deeper. Girls sure had odd ways of doing things. Yet not all girls were like Karo-chan. "Never believe people who try to tell you that boys are a certain way, but girls are entirely different," Great-grandpa was always saying. There were various types of girls. Mumei remembered the little girl next door. She looked mysterious, with her eyes so far apart. He was thinking how anxious he was to get home so he could see her face again when Yasukawamaru yelled, "Mr. Yonatani, I want to go to the outhouse."

"Me too!"

"Me too!"

After considering the state of his bladder, Mumei decided he didn't need to go. Even so, watching the heads of the other kids bob as they filed out of the classroom he found himself drawn toward them.

That reminded him of something Great-grandpa had said about words. He mustn't copy kids he heard using foreign words like *peppy* or *potty*, but *peebuddy*—Great-grandpa had laughed when he said it—was entirely different, a word even the most extreme nationalist would accept as bona fide Japanese, so he should feel free to use it; besides, when you went for a pee with your friends, you all got caught up in the flow, so it was really the best time to let your hair down and have a good talk.

All those words—dead ones and the ones that weren't quite dead but that nobody ever used anymore—were stored in Great-grandpa's head. He was always wanting to throw out old crockery or toys they didn't use anymore, yet he kept all the old useless words in the drawers of his brain, never letting them go.

He'd heard about a time when girls and boys went to different schools. After that, they went to the same school but the outhouse, which was then called the toilet, and gym class, were kept separate—sort of a neither-here-nor-there situation. Then boys and girls had gym together, but the toilets were still separate. That had been phased out as the differences between the sexes became less and less clear.

Toilet sounded to Mumei like *toil*, but since it wasn't a place where you went to work, he sensed a contradiction in the word. But then again, it had apparently come from English, so maybe *toil* and *toilet* had nothing to do with each other after all.

The outhouse in Mumei's school, used by both girls and boys, was a joyful place, filled with bright colors: red, yellow, blue, green. You could have a nice leisurely poop squatted on top of a lotus flower, or choose a chrysanthemum from the flowerbed on the wall to spray with your pee. Long ago, the toilet wasn't a place to play—you were supposed to do your business and get out as soon as possible. People who spent a long time in the toilet were suspected of doing something wrong on the sly. This was probably to reduce contact with harmful germs, but for some time now people had stopped worrying about coliform bacteria. The human body knew how to deal with them. Mr. Yonatani always assured them that there were plenty of things a lot more frightening in their environment now.

"It's the Malaysian Peninsula," Mumei said to Yanagi-kun, who was standing next to him, struggling to open his fly.

"What is?" Yanagi-kun asked, sounding bored as he continued to fight with his zipper.

"What you're trying to get out," giggled Mumei. A map of the world was plastered to the interior of Mumei's forehead, making objects in front of him sometimes resemble faraway peninsulas or mountain ranges. The Malaysian Peninsula apparently didn't mean much to Yanagi-kun, though.

The trousers Yoshiro had made especially for Mumei didn't have either a zipper or buttons. The front was hidden by two pieces of cloth on the left and right that neatly overlapped. Yoshiro had only started sewing when he was in his eighties, but being an enthusiastic learner he'd quickly progressed to the point where he now made clothes with collars and sleeves so ingeniously crafted that Mumei was almost embarrassed to wear them. He'd been hoping no one would notice when Tatsugoro-kun looked over and shouted, "Hey, that's really cool! Let me see." Suddenly, all the kids were staring at him. Tatsugoro-kun said he wanted to be an artist specializing in clothing. In olden times, people who did that sort of work were called designers—a very popular profession, apparently. Tatsugoro didn't want to be rich or famous; he simply wanted to make the bizarre clothing that appeared to him in dreams, and see people actually wearing it. Once he'd asked Mumei, "Wouldn't you like a suit that turned you into a cicada the minute you put it on? All you'd have to do is flutter the sleeves and they'd chirr like a cicada. Awesome, huh?" Thinking that sounded a little too scary, Mumei had declined the offer. Another time the kid had asked, "How about a pair of trousers with a hundred pockets?" With that many what would you put in them all, he had wanted to know. Pencils, erasers, candy, marbles, tickets, pills, Tatsu-goro replied—there'd be a special pocket for everything you could think of.

While the children were talking, the three gentlemen on this month's Outhouse Cleaning Brigade came in. They were laughing and joking, discussing something as they peered into a test tube filled with liquid the color of a green tree frog. One had been a chemistry professor at the university, another had worked for a major pharmaceutical firm, while the third never spoke of his past. Because Mumei and his classmates weren't strong enough to clean the outhouse, the young-elderly elite volunteered for this duty. Perhaps just cleaning wasn't enough to satisfy them, for they were always developing new tools and antiseptics—research they funded them-selves—which they then donated to the school. Seeing them always embarrassed Mumei, as if someone had seen his pee or poo, so he always tried to get away as soon as he could.

One time Yanagi-kun had run straight into this trio of elites on his way out of the outhouse. His whole body stiff, he had bowed deeply and said, "You are doing an excellent job." Watching from a short distance away, Mumei had been terribly impressed and, wondering where Yanagi-kun had learned that expression, raised his hand in a class where they were discussing greetings to report what he'd heard.

"'You are doing an excellent job' is something an employer says to the people working for him," Mr. Yonatani had ex-plained, somewhat nonplussed. "Those men aren't your em-ployees, are they?"

Blushing to the roots of his ears, Yanagi-kun had asked, "So what should I say?"

"*Excuse me* is what you say," offered Kama-chan enthusiastically.

Placing his hand lightly on her shoulder, Yonatani said, "*Excuse me* is what you say when you want to apologize for something. A long time ago it was also used to express gratitude, but you mustn't apologize when you haven't done anything wrong."

"But we're putting them to a lot of trouble."

"We don't talk about *putting people to a lot of trouble* anymore—that expression is dead. A long time ago, when civilization hadn't progressed to where it is now, there used to be a distinction between useful and useless people. You children mustn't carry on that way of thinking."

"Didn't people used to say *arigato*?"

"*Arigato*—sounds crunchy, but kind of sweet, too."

"That word is also dead."

Just then, one of the boys yelled, "Graaaaateful," loud enough to make himself hoarse. Laughter bubbled up from the bottoms of the children's feet until the whole room was seething like a pot come to the boil. "Ahem!" Yonatani dramatically cleared his throat. "These days it's popular to shout *graaaateful* as an expression of thanks," he went on, "but don't you think it might sound strange to the young elderly, the middle-aged elderly, and most of all to the aged elderly? It makes them uncomfortable, don't you see?"

"No weeeeee don't," the kids screamed back in perfect unison, not that they'd discussed which vowel to draw out ahead of time. Yonatani wondered how they managed that, noting that he probably would have chosen the *o* of "no" rather than the *e* of "we." Could it be that each generation has its own sense of rhythm?

"Mama said something like that the last time she came for a visit," Tatsugoro said, his brow furrowed. "*Graaaateful* sounds weird, she said."

"You still say *Mama*? You're really behind the times," teased Yanagi-kun. Tatsugoro's mother had mixed the old-fashioned word *Mama* in with his formula when he was a baby. Now that they no longer lived together, he still heard *Mama* whispering softly to him from somewhere in his inner ear. Enraged at Yanagi-kun for laughing at *Mama*, Tatsugoro pounced.

"A fight, a fight, let's go watch," Mumei chanted as if reading from a script, prompting the two boys to stop tussling and look over at him, wearily rolling their eyes. What Mr. Yonatani said next made them forget all about their feud.

"You know, *arigato* was a pretty good word after all. When we think of ordinary things as *arigatai*—very rare, or special, we see them with a new sense of wonder and gratitude. *Arigato*." As soon as he said them, though, Yonatani lost confidence in his own words. With all the old ways turning flips, it was getting harder and harder for adults to say to children, "Do this and you'll never go wrong." Kids didn't trust a grown-up who seemed too cocksure—they were more willing to listen if he didn't hide his lack of confidence. All he could do was feel his way forward, unsure of the way, thinking carefully about each new thing he encountered, turning every doubt into words to give to his pupils. But as soon as the uncertainty became unbearable, causing his voice to waver and trail off, the classroom would get as noisy as a beehive whacked by a stick. He'd have to do something before things got out of hand. Suddenly it came to him—he knew just what to do.

Yonatani went to the closet at the back of the room and slid the creaky door open. Mumei's heart, seized by a ticklish sense of expectation, beat faster. In his hand, the teacher held a pole six feet long with a map of the world wrapped around it, which he unfurled in front of the blackboard. Thrusting both hands in the air, Mumei jumped straight up, shouting, "Paradise!" The other kids stopped chattering and moved to sit around the map in a semicircle. Mumei wasn't the only one who loved this map of the world. Catching the wind, the map turned into the sail of a huge sailboat; breathing in the salt air, listening to the lapping of the waves, they swayed gently back and forth to the rhythm as the sea breeze ruffled their hair and the cries of seagulls split the air.

"This is where you are now," said Yonatani, placing the long nail of his index finger on the center of the Seahorse Archipelago. The map was covered with brown stains. Straining to see which were islands and which were brown spots, Mumei edged his way closer, moving first his left knee, then his right.

"Long, long ago, the Japanese archipelago was a peninsula, attached to the continent, until it was thrown off to become an archipelago. And until just recently it was still much closer to the continent, but the last big earthquake left a deep crevice in the seabed, pushing our archipelago much farther away. This map was made before that happened. Since then, a number of large-scale observation and research projects have been undertaken, but none seem likely to be completed anytime soon. The government says that a new map can't be made due to a lack of funds, and is trying to push through a new tax called the cartography tax. Due to the greater distance from the continent, many changes have taken place in Japan's climate and culture."

Yonatani wasn't sure how long it had been since he'd started talking to children just as he did to adults. The kids could catch the general meaning without a dictionary so long as new words were mixed in with lots of others they already knew. If about ten per cent of the words in everything they read were unfamiliar, their vocabularies would keep on growing. All he could teach them was how to cultivate language. He was hoping they themselves would plant, harvest, consume, and grow fat on words.

With eyes like grapes moist with dew, the children stared up at the map of the world, never tiring of Yonatani's stories about countries beyond the sea. From among these kids he would have to find the one most suitable to be an emissary. Because his work involved constant observation of lots of elementary school pupils, Yonatani considered this to be his mission. For the time being he had his eye on Mumei, though he would have to watch him mature over the next several years before making a final decision.

Mumei blinked furiously. He felt a stabbing pain in the core of his brain. The pounding of his heart had shifted from his chest to his inner ears. He caught a whiff of blood from somewhere in the back of his nose. But he knew that if he said he wasn't feeling well the teacher might end the geography lesson, so he swallowed hard again and again, clenched his fists, and endured.

To Mumei, the map of the world was starting to look like an x-ray of his own internal organs. On his right side was the American continent, with Eurasia on the left. In his gut he could feel Australia. What was it Mr. Yonatani said just now? That the Japanese archipelago was once attached to the continent? How could that be? That it used to be a peninsula? Did that mean that a long time ago you could walk to the continent, cross tracts of land so broad you could feel the roundness of the earth, striding so far it made you dizzy just to think of it?

"Why were we sent so far away from the continent?" someone asked. Wondering who that was, Mumei tried to turn his head but his neck was so stiff he couldn't move.

"My great-grandpa says Japan did something really bad so now the continent hates us," said Tatsugoro, sounding pleased with himself; Yonatani nodded with a rueful laugh.

"Look. See this big ocean in the middle of the world? It's called the Pacific Ocean. To the left of it are Eurasia and Africa; on the right are the Americas. The huge plates at the bottom of the Pacific Ocean shift sometimes. When that happens, at the edge of the plates there's a big earthquake, and sometimes a tsunami. There's nothing human beings can do to prevent it. That's just the way the earth is. But Japan isn't the way it is now just because of earthquakes and tsunami. If natural disasters were the only problem, we certainly would have recovered long before now. So it's not just natural disasters. Got that?"

As soon as Yonatani said that, the fire alarm started clanging loudly. Yonatani walked over to the red machine to turn off the switch.

The next thing Mumei knew he was saying, "The earth's round, you know," in a gentle voice that carried well all the same. He hadn't known what he wanted to say: the words just came out on their own. The other kids gave him puzzled looks. Mumei started to flap both his arms like the wings of a bird. He simply didn't know what else to do, though to the others it looked like he was fooling around, imitating a crane. The teacher's eyes narrowed in a smile. "Yes, that's right. The earth is round," he said, "This map is a flat drawing of a sphere. I'd forgotten to tell you that." He pretended to scratch his head in embarrassment.

"Round? What do you mean? So this map's a lie?" Yasu-kawamaru shouted, angry at having been betrayed.

"So that's it. Round, huh?" Tatsugoro, too, was dumb-founded.

Yonatani didn't know how to answer them. He hadn't meant to trick them. What he'd wanted to tell them seemed more important than the fact that the earth is round. Yet perhaps the shape of the earth was important, too.

"Later on let's cut up some paper and make a globe, like a ball."

Bearing up under the pain of the two awls digging into his head from either side, Mumei flapped his arms like crazy. It was strange how none of the others could see what he was doing. The more isolated he felt the blurrier everything got, so he tried to focus on the map, staring at it until creases formed in his forehead. This map is definitely my portrait, he thought. The Andes Mountains curve outward then inward again, just like the bone of my right leg from my hip to my ankle. The bones in my torso curve inward toward the top, until they meet that mountain range rising from the left at the Bering Sea. All my bones are curved. Not that I bent them, they were just like that to begin with—if this is what's called pain, it was there from the start, for no particular reason. Water from a melted Arctic glacier; the cold ocean; my brain. The earth is full of complicated wrinkles. My lungs are the Gobi Desert; the stretched-out palm next to it is Europe. The African continent has a big, broad chest but small hips. It's like a dancer standing on one leg. My neck, which connects Africa to Europe, is twisted, with swollen thyroid and swollen tonsils, screaming for help. Australia is my gut, a big bag. There's lots of food in the bag. But I can't eat any of it.

"See? Maps of the world made in Japan always have the Pacific Ocean in the center, with the Americas on the right, while Eurasia and Africa are on the left. But if you cut the globe in a different way, when you open it up, you'll get a different map of the world," Mr. Yonatani said, looking around at the children's faces. Mumei gasped. For a moment his body was released from the pain of overlapping with this map of the world. He now knew there were other, different maps. The teacher went on.

"There's a trench beneath the sea that circles the Pacific Ocean like a ring. It runs up the coast of South America, then further north alongside California where it turns left to cross Alaska, then from Kamchatka it sweeps down to the Mariana Islands, forming a huge ring. The Japanese archipelago sits on top of this ring. There's a bit of a dent in the ring now, along the eastern coast of Japan."

"About how many glasses of water are there in the Pacific Ocean?" Yanagi-kun blurted out.

While the kids laughed, Yonatani looked straight ahead, not even lifting an eyebrow as he answered, "Water may spill out during earthquakes, so maybe there's less than there used to be."

"That's a lie! Mr. Yonatani tells lies!" shouted Kama-chan. At that moment, Mumei felt the trembling of the earth in the whorl of his hair as water from the Pacific Ocean splattered out into the universe. His arms and fingers went into spasms. If he went on quivering this way his bones and flesh would melt into drops that spattered out in all four directions, but what could he do? He couldn't stop it. The eyes and mouths that surrounded him were round O's of surprise though he couldn't tell who was who, nor could he speak. He watched his teacher's face spread out like ripples, growing larger and larger, with nothing beyond it but darkness.

The street was made of glass sheeting. Below it was a seemingly bottomless cavern. The glass was said to be strong enough to withstand considerable stress; if it did crack, though, how far would one fall? When it was discovered that the contamination permeating the soil had seeped into the asphalt that covered the streets, citizens protested to the government, which refused to conduct an investigation to find out who was responsible, leaving the matter to the local authorities, which hired professionals to dig out the contaminated earth deep below the asphalt, then paid contractors to haul it away and place these thick glass sheets over the hole to keep pedestrians from falling into the depths of hell. People preferred not to know what the contractors had done with the contaminated earth. A conscientious newspaper reporter found out that they had sold it to the government. But what had the government done with all the dirt they had paid so much money for? The public reacted to a dodgy explanation offered by an official from the Ministry of Environmental Pollution—that it had been carried outside the solar system by a private spaceship where it had been duly discarded—with derision. For many nights the sky was full of stars laughing coldly down on them. Some worried that the moon had absconded in disgust. Fortunately, it reappeared a while later, looking exhausted.

The night the moon came back, the breasts of young boys grew round and firm while the fragrance of ripe figs wafted up from between their legs, thrown wide apart, their knees raised slightly as they slept. Mumei, too, awoke to a sweet aroma and, realizing that his sheets were damp, got out of bed to discover that red juice had left a large stain. Feeling as if someone were watching him, he flung the curtains open to find a huge, yellow full moon, low in the sky, staring at him. Why was the moon so big tonight? Did it just look big and fuzzy because his eyes had gotten weaker? Maybe he needed glasses. No, he already had a pair. He could see them, over there on his desk. Mumei knew that he was now fifteen years old. He clearly remembered fainting one day when he was in elementary school while looking at a map of the world. At that moment, he had apparently leaped across time, propelled into the future. Even so, this self felt right. It fit him nicely, without the excess folds there would be, say, in a coat that was too big for him. As watching the moon made his eyelids heavy he let them close, then opened them to find it was morning. He took off his pajamas, changed into an azure silk costume with a thin magenta necktie, and put on his glasses. Sitting in his wheelchair, he went outside. The glass beneath his wheels reflected the seven colors of the spectrum in the morning light like a soap bubble. Mumei glided smoothly down the road like an ice skater. The control ball read his thoughts through his fingers, turning the wheelchair to the right or stopping it as he wished. Though in elementary school Mumei had been able to walk a little on his own, as he matured moving his legs had become more and more difficult until he could no longer even stand up for very long. Realizing that this fifteen-year-old self couldn't walk at all didn't particularly surprise him. As soon as his desire to go diagonally to the right traveled from his abdomen to his fingers, the control ball at the end of the armrest responded to the slight pressure, sending the wheelchair in that direction.

"Ah." Mumei tested his voice. It came from his wristwatch, not his vocal cords. It sounded gentle and young, yet it was a voice you could depend on—warm, bright, and full of life. He wasn't sure how reliable a breathing machine would be, though. Soon he would have to leave the task of breathing to a machine outside his body, which he would have to keep by him in order to live. What would happen to the machine if his wheelchair fell over? Needing someone to help him twenty-four hours a day would be an awful nuisance. Mumei liked going out alone, riding the wheelchair down a steep hill so that it would turn it over with him in it. After being thrown out of the chair, he would lie on his back looking up at the sky. For how many more years would he be able to enjoy these daring excursions?

Falling out of the chair when it turned over didn't frighten him at all. He wasn't heavy enough to break the glass, and was so adept at curling up to take the impact that he had never broken a bone. The moment the chair fell, its warning buzzer automatically contacted the Women's Rescue Brigade, bringing a squad of young-elderly aunties to help him. While waiting for them, he reveled in the pure joy of having been tossed out onto the earth's surface. Unwilling to let him go, gravity tugged at him so he wouldn't float off into space. Gazing up at the sky, he breathed in and out. There was nothing to worry about. Mumei's generation was equipped with natural defenses against despair. As always, it was the elderly they had to feel sorry for. At the age of 115, Yoshiro was still spry enough to rent a dog for a run every morning, then squeeze an orange for Mumei's juice, cut up his vegetables, stroll through the market with his knapsack, wipe the window sash and on top of the dresser with a wrung-out mop-up cloth before the dust had time to settle, write a picture postcard to his daughter, briskly scrub the underwear he'd left to soak in a pail overnight, then take out his sewing basket in the evenings to fashion smart new clothes for his great-grandson. Why this frenzy of never-ending work? To stave off an endless stream of tears.

Mumei took a long ticket with a picture of an ocean liner out of his pocket. Having skipped over several years, he wasn't quite sure what he was doing with it, though it seemed familiar in a way. He closed his eyes and steadied his breathing, trying to remember. In time, wisps of memory came back from the future. Having been chosen as an emissary, he was to stow away on a ship bound for Madras, India. There, an international medical research institute would be waiting for him. Data about his health would be used for medical research that would help people the world over as well as, perhaps, making it possible for Mumei to live longer.

It was Mr. Yonatani, his homeroom teacher in elementary school, who had approached him about becoming an emissary. Mumei hadn't heard from him for years when sometime after his fifteenth birthday, his old teacher suddenly appeared on their doorstep. Yoshiro had been as surprised as Mumei; after the three had chatted a while, Yonatani had taken only Mumei out for a meal. Shown to a small room without windows in a high-class restaurant specializing in walnut cooking, they had sat and talked for three hours. Yonatani began by telling Mumei about his own childhood.

Mr. Yonatani's father's, whose surname was Yonatan, had disappeared soon after his marriage. Though his mother was so attached to the name Yonatan that she wanted to keep it as her own, at a time when having non-Japanese relatives was enough to bring you under suspicion, such a foreign-sounding surname was sure to be a strike against her. She did, in fact, often feel she was being watched. She would come home to find signs of a break-in; even when nothing had been taken, the police would come round to investigate. She changed her name to Yonatani, writing it in Chinese characters, and raised the boy on her own, shielding him with her strong arms, never mentioning his father. Hearing this made Mumei notice certain things about his teacher's face for the first time. His prominent nose descended directly from a high ridge between his eyes. His cheekbones, on the other hand, were not particularly conspicuous. He had deep set eyes, and a long, thin face, with hollow cheeks and a long jaw.

It was during this conversation that Mumei first heard the word *emissary*. In hushed tones, Yonatani explained that even though it couldn't be made public, the plan to send emissaries abroad was not so forbidden as to be considered a crime, so he shouldn't let it scare him. People caught stowing away on ships sometimes spent several days in custody, but so far, none had actually been punished. Officially, the purpose of the isolation policy was to suppress any attempt to sway the public toward opening the country, not to place legal restrictions on individual travel. Even if this was true, however, government policy could change overnight. A person might be sentenced to life in prison next week for doing something no one would even notice today. That was why members of the "Emissary Association" Yonatani belonged to were determined to find a suitable candidate and send him or her abroad now, before the government changed its mind. This would make it possible to thoroughly research the state of Japanese children's health, yielding information that would prove useful if similar phenomena began to appear in other countries. It was clearly necessary to think of the future along the curved lines of our round earth. The isolation policy that looked so invulnerable was actually nothing but a sand castle. You could destroy it, little by little, with those plastic shovels kids use at the beach. The Emissary Association planned to start the process as private citizens, sending promising young people overseas, one after another.

The Emissary Association was unknown to the general public: there was no newsletter, nor did its members gather for large conferences. At most, three or four would meet at someone's house. There were no dues or membership cards. Headquarters was on the small island of Shikoku, spread out over eighty-eight different sites, making it extremely difficult to determine the exact location. Was there a way to tell members by sight? Mumei wanted to know. No, not really, Yonatani told him. Yet there was a ritual members performed by themselves to reaffirm their sense of membership. They all got up before dawn to light a candle which they took with them when they entered the darkness before beginning their day's work. The candle had to be exactly two inches in diameter and four inches tall.

According to Yonatani's explanation, at the appointed time Mumei was to go to the pier at Yokohama Port that had a sign saying "International Traveler's Terminal." A border patrol boat with a green stripe along its belly would be waiting for him; when a man in uniform appeared he was to show him his ticket and ask where to go. If the man said, "Board this boat for the time being," he was to do so without hesitation. The boat would carry him out to sea, where he would be transferred to a foreign ship. Certain that of all the pupils he'd taught none was more suitable to be an emissary than Mumei, Yonatani had kept his eye on him since he had finished elementary school, asking about him, and watching him grow up from afar.

Sure that at age fifteen Mumei was psychologically mature enough, and knowing he would soon have to breathe through a machine, which would complicate matters, Yonatani had decided to approach the boy directly. Of course he could refuse, or wait a little longer, Yonatani assured him, blue veins standing out at his temples.

"I understand. I'll go right away."

Mumei's voice, which would never change, was high and clear.

They agreed to meet at the same place the next day, but on the way home, thinking of his great-grandfather, Mumei's resolve began to waver. Through the years, they had grown even closer than before. Fragments, scenes from that time he was supposed to have skipped over now came back to him. The Silver-Headed League, for instance. What would become of the Silver-Headed League if he were to leave? It must have been three years before that Mumei's hair had lost all its color, turning a gleaming silver almost overnight.

Looking at himself in the mirror, Mumei had said, hoping to make Yoshiro smile, "We're like twins with hair the same color!" But Yoshiro had wept, holding his great-grandson tightly to his chest, gently stroking his head. When Mumei quickly blurted out, "Great-grandpa, let's form a Silver-Headed League, just the two of us. Our hair will be our membership card. You've done just fine with silver hair for over fifty years, so I'll be fine, too, for at least another fifty," Yoshiro's tears had stopped like a miracle as a silver smile flashed in the corners of his eyes.

One day the Nemoto woman from next door had suddenly moved away, taking Suiren with her. Mumei, though still a child, had known for some time that Yoshiro was in love with her. She didn't leave an address, nor did she contact him, not even once. Though he had looked down in the mouth for a time, Mumei vaguely remembered him saying, "Must have had to go into hiding. Special circumstances … It'll be lonely without them, but I've still got you …" Yoshiro's weary-looking back gradually straightened up again, and the color came back to his cheeks. Mumei, too, felt empty when Suiren disappeared, as if there was a hole somewhere inside him, but, spreading his fingers, he released the despair burning the palm of his hand. Or perhaps without really understanding them, he simply accepted the *special circumstances* that surrounded them all like a spider's web.

That morning when Mumei, still in second grade, first became aware of Suiren, Yoshiro was heading for home, pushing the handlebars of his bike like the horns of a stubborn water buffalo. Having angrily thrown off its veil of thin clouds, the sun now pounded down on his forehead. Everything he saw seemed to exude pain or trouble; even innocent telegraph poles cut the sky up with meaningless vertical lines just to defy him. Some terrible mistake he had made long ago—the memory of it eluded him—kept scratching at his insides. That deadly error had landed them all in prison, and the telegraph poles were bars on the windows, telling him every morning that he would never reach the magical land beyond. How wonderful it would be to leave his grandson to his daughter, his great-grandson to his grandson, and fly there, across the sky. This was not hope, it was anger. To keep his rage from splitting his heart open, he opened his mouth and laughed as loud as he could, but even that failed to cheer him up.

In the old days, everyone strolled across the street as soon as the traffic light changed from red to green. Back then people used to call the green light "blue." Blue was the color of fresh vegetables, of grassy fields. Oh, and sometimes even Sundays. Not green. Blue. Azure. The color of the sea, the fields, the sky. Not green. Or clean. Green, clean. Clean politics? No, never! "Clean" means antiseptic, some chemical they use to kill off whoever they decide are no better than human germs. City Hall officials are offal, the way they skulk around, messing up laws. I'd like to scoop them up like dog shit. My great-grandson wants to have a picnic, in a field. Whose fault is it that I can't make even a little dream like that come true, why are all the fields contaminated? And what're you going to do about it? Wealth, prestige, none of it has the value of a single blade of grass. You hear me, listen, LISTEN, get a Q-tip, dig all those lousy excuses out of your ears, and hear me out! Yoshiro's thoughts were interrupted by a stone that flew up from the front wheel of his bicycle to catch him in the shin. "Ouch!" On the verge of screaming "Shit, shit, shit," he swallowed hard, forcing the words down along with his saliva, then realizing too late that Mumei wasn't there, making it all right to spew out foul language if only he hadn't lost the heart by that time. "How short my fuse has gotten," he thought, "I'm covered in verbal filth." Without Mumei in his life, everything would be stinking from all the rottenness.

When he got home, he saw the house next door, outlined sharply against the sky. He went around to the south side, only to find all the curtains shut. He gave up and went home, where he sat down on a folding chair to work on the piece he was writing. That was when he heard the disturbing sound of wings flapping outside. Must be a carrier pigeon, he thought, getting up to open a window. Seeing a dark shadow cross the yard, he ran outside barefoot. The solar-powered carrier pigeon flew as it was programmed to, circling Yoshiro's house three times before landing in the entrance way. The bird's eyes, shiny as black pearls, were terrifying. He took the letter out of the small gold tube attached to its thin leg, spread it out, and read it: Mumei had fainted in class and was now being examined by the doctor.

Fifteen-year-old Mumei saw another wheelchair, coming this way. In it sat a girl about his own age, with shining silver hair. Thinking of asking her to join the Silver-Headed League, he smiled at her, the sweetest smile he could manage. The girl stopped in front of him, blinking at him with a puzzled sort of look. He inched toward her at the speed of a snail. The nearer he got, the more deeply mysterious her face became. Her eyes were further apart than most people's. Though probably dark, depending on the angle of the sun they could take on an azure shine. Noticing that she was looking at the area around his stomach, Mumei quickly glanced down. Nothing seemed to be out of the ordinary. Yet though he couldn't see it, through his loose-fitting clothes he felt something like a warm ball in his lap.

Mumei passed the girl, then immediately changed direction so that their wheelchairs were side by side, facing in the same direction. Facing each other, it seemed to him, they'd be too far away to talk.

"It's been a long time," the girl said. Eh? Startled, Mumei stuck out his chin and turned his head to stare at the girl, who now had her head turned at exactly the same angle; as soon as their eyes met, he felt himself being drawn into the space between hers.

"Are you the girl who used to live next door?"

"You remember me?"

"You went away so suddenly, I was wondering what happened to you."

"There were special circumstances."

There was a brief pause.

"Do you have some time? Let's go down to the sea."

Suiren nodded, and the two propelled their wheelchairs smoothly down the glass road side by side. Why was the ocean this close? Mumei wondered. Had the island of Honshu gotten this narrow? These doubts faded from his brain almost as soon as they entered it. When a steep slope appeared on their right, Mumei put on some speed, heading straight down without putting on the brake. The chair sank into the sand at the bottom, falling over, throwing Mumei out onto the beach. Breathing heavily, he shouted to the girl, still at the top of the hill, "Come on, try it!" Suiren's wheelchair started rolling down the slope. It picked up speed, and as soon as the wheels hit the sand, Suiren threw her weight over to the side so she'd fall beside Mumei. The waves broke several times before her breathing returned to normal.

"If I were to cross the sea, would you come with me?" asked Suiren. Mumei was too surprised to answer right away. Her brow furrowed, Suiren sighed, "I was thinking that you were as curious about the world as I am, but I guess I'm wrong. You're scared. Well, never mind, I'll go alone."

Mumei quickly blurted out, "Oh, of course I'll go with you, but ..."

For the very first time, Mumei cooked up what you might call a strategy. He quickly buried the words "I was planning to go alone, too" deep in the sand. If he didn't tell her that, Suiren might think he had made up his mind to leave his old life behind just for her.

The hot sand smelled like seaweed, and when the moist air sticking to their skin mixed with their sweat, touching their lips, it tasted salty. The waves sounded so close, yet lifting their heads, they saw the sea was further away than they'd thought. Mumei's consciousness traveled downward; the moment it reached his crotch, warmed from beneath by the sand, his heart stopped. Something between his legs was changing. He was turning into a woman. Sand made of bits of broken seashells stuck to Suiren's forehead, shining in the sunlight. Was she still a girl? Or was she turning into a boy? She had the face of a beautiful woman, but these days there were plenty of boys who looked like that. Pursing her lips, raising her eyebrows ever so slightly, she gave him a come-hither look. He couldn't hear what she was saying, but when he tried to sit up for a better look at her lips, he was held back by the sand, unable to move. Thrusting first his left shoulder out, then his right, he tried to get up. Suiren was already in a sitting position, her back straight. Her face blotted out Mumei's sky. There was a space between her eyes. Her right eye, her left eye. They blurred, spreading out into blotches. The two big spots side by side weren't eyes but a pair of lungs. No, not lungs, they were two huge broad beans. No, not beans, but human faces. The one on the left was Mr. Yonatani; Great-grandpa was on the right. Both faces were twisted with worry. He wanted to say, "I'm all right. I just had a really nice dream," but his tongue wouldn't move. If only he could smile at least, to reassure them. That's what he was thinking when darkness, wearing a glove, reached for the back of his head to take hold of his brains, and Mumei fell into the pitch-black depths of the strait.